THE APARTMENT ACROSS THE HALL

THE APARTMENT ACROSS THE HALL

A PSYCHOLOGICAL THRILLER

JACK DANE

CONTENTS

ABOUT THE APARTMENT ACROSS THE HALL

They say you can't pick your neighbors... but can you survive them?

When Salem Ripley moves into her apartment in New York City, she's disheartened to find it isn't exactly like the pictures. Still, with her past, she's lucky to find a place at all.

Her neighbor across the hall is tall, dark and handsome. After seeing his beautiful girlfriend, Salem can't help but obsess over the couple and their perfect life.

Then Salem sees her neighbor with another girl. And another. And another. The strangest part? **She never sees the women leave**.

Salem should ignore it.. After all, it's really none of her business. But she can't shake the strange feeling that something is wrong–and that lives are at stake. She has no choice–she has to find out **what's going on in the apartment across the hall**…

A note from the author: Thank you for picking up my book! I know how valuable reading time is, and I really hope you'll enjoy the story.

Happy reading,

Jack

PROLOGUE

The pounding at the door starts up again.

It's the police, wanting to get in. I can hear their voices as they call out to me through the thick wood of the old door.

Another fist thuds down, but my brain tunes it out so that it's little more than background noise as my eyes drift to the wall across from me.

Blood is everywhere. It stains the framed pictures of minimalist art, the splattered red running down like tiny river streams before it pools between the old floor tiles.

The cops shout again, their calls frantic as they knock hard.

Even though I know I should open the door, I'm frozen to the spot. My feet won't move. Can't move.

When they come inside, everything will change.

The small window to my left lets in a cool fall breeze, the cold air wafting over my sweat-soaked face and rustling my hair.

My eyes follow the trails of blood down the wall, tracing every inch of red stains before finally my gaze settles on the body itself.

Here, there's even more blood. Pools of it, the dark liquid sinking deep into every crevice.

I hear the policemen's insistent commands to open the door, but only distantly. I can't pull my eyes away from the body.

So still.

The doorframe shakes as another thunderous boom echoes out in the dingy apartment. Soon, they'll be inside.

Another breeze touches my skin, drawing my head to the open window.

Almost in a trance, I stand slowly and begin taking careful steps toward the window as the cops break through the door behind me.

The wood splinters under the constant assault. I hear them shout my name, but my head doesn't turn.

I reach the window and lower my forehead to it, taking a deep, shaking breath as I peer down to the alleyway below. The glass is cool against my skin.

No doubt there will be alarm when they see the body on the floor.

I just wonder what they'll say when they find out there's another one on the ground outside the window, too.

CHAPTER 1

ne week earlier

O I look up at the ancient brick and stone walk-up before me as a brisk October wind blasts my face.

It's cold enough to feel like a slap on my eyeballs, forcing me to squint a little as my eyes tear up. I've got my heavy-duty trench coat buttoned all the way up, but it isn't really enough.

Fall in New York City is a strange thing. One second, it's eighty degrees and so hot you're practically begging for death, and then the next day you wake up to find the leaves are orange and the air wants to hurt you.

Not exactly the perfect time to move.

As if I had a choice. My lease was up, and I certainly don't make enough to re-sign considering what the landlord wanted to charge me. So that meant packing up my meager belongings and beginning the tireless search for a new place to stay.

I'd wanted to stay in Manhattan, but that just didn't seem to be in the cards. After a fruitless patrol of every apartment listing imaginable, it was clear the island is just too pricey for me these days. Even Brooklyn was starting to look hopeless until Derek found this place in Williamsburg.

"You got the keys?"

I turn to Derek standing beside me on the street, my heaviest suitcase hoisted over his shoulder. It's a monstrosity of a case, and practically bursting at the seams with all the stuff I've got packed into it, but he doesn't seem to be struggling.

I nod and dive into the pockets of my trench coat in search of the key before pulling it out to hold it up in a shivering hand.

Derek flashes a grin. "You owe me big time for finding this place, Sal."

I grin as the wind blows again, making my smile falter a little as the breeze cuts through me.

"Whatever flavor of ramen you want–it's on me."

Derek rolls his eyes as he adjusts the suitcase. "Gee, thanks."

It's true though–I really do owe him. If it wasn't for him, I would've never found this place.

It hadn't appeared on any listing sites, which was unfortunately all too common in a place like NYC. "Knowing a guy" was definitely beneficial here.

As a garbage man, Derek sees a lot of the city. This place is on his route, and when he heard of my plight, he suggested I give it a shot.

With my history, I didn't think I'd have much of a shot of my application getting accepted. I didn't think I'd have much of a shot getting accepted anywhere, to be completely honest.

By some small miracle, they let me in.

"Sal—as much as I love freezing my balls off on the street, how about we go inside?" Derek asks, pulling me from my thoughts.

I nod and turn to the door.

We aren't far from the subway, only about a five-minute walk. It's a good thing too, because I can't afford Ubers.

I grab hold of the two wheeled suitcases I've been pulling along and make my way up to the front gate.

It's rusty, but someone has slapped a coat of black paint on top of the rust like that'll fix it.

Whatever. At least I have a place to sleep that isn't the street.

I grab the knob and turn it.

The gate lets out a squeak as it swings open to allow us access to the three stone steps leading up to a metal door.

The door is also painted black, though it's in dire need of a new coat of paint itself. A chip on one side allows me to see just how many layers of paint this thing actually wears, each coat like a layer of sediment in the Earth.

"Come on, Sal," Derek says from behind me.

Finally, he's showing some signs of strain. He ought to— I've got everything I own in these three suitcases.

My hand shakes a little as I work the key into the lock, an effect of excitement and the chilly temperature.

With a heavy click, the door opens.

"Finally," Derek says with a sigh.

I slip inside, finding myself in a small, tiled entryway. The paint is peeling off the walls, which at one time had been white. It's faded now, with a couple of mysterious stains in various shades of yellow and brown that I don't really want to stare too long at.

Another door stands open in front of us, but this one isn't locked. I push it open with ease.

Despite the shoddy state of the place, at least we're finally out of the wind.

Our breathing seems to echo a little in the quiet hall as we come fully inside.

"It's… homey," Derek offers with a grin.

The tile from the entryway continues through here before disappearing around the staircase at the end of the hall. At the base of the wall is a painted black trim, scarred by myriad scuffs and scratches picked up over the years.

Patches of paint are missing from the ceiling, too.

It's beginning to make a lot of sense why this place actually accepted my application, despite the glaring red flags that no doubt showed up on my background check.

Oh well. Good thing I'm not picky.

A loud thud makes me jump.

I whirl around, heart beating, only to find that the door has finally shut behind us.

Derek chuckles at my fright. "You okay?"

"Fine. Just caught me off guard, that's all."

I don't tell him that my hands have broken out into a sweat, or that my mind races wildly with thoughts that threaten to overwhelm me.

If only he knew.

"Which unit are you?" asks Derek.

I look down at my phone to the email I've got pulled up.

"Um… Five B."

We start the march forward, our footsteps on the tile echoing as we go.

The first apartment is on the left, the door painted a dull gray. Just below the peephole is an oxidized bronze *1A*. The second apartment is a couple feet further down and on the right, with a *1B* across it's door.

A few more steps, and we're at the base of the stairs.

Derek looks over a small bulletin board hanging above the painted-over radiator to our right.

The sheets of paper stuck to it are varying shades of pink, yellow and white. Most of them are curled and look as if they've been up there for years.

PLEASE DO NOT LEAVE PACKAGES ON RADIATOR one page reads, the typed text printed large on the paper.

In front of me are the doors to two more apartments, separated by only a few inches of cracked white wall between the trim.

I step forward, making my way over to the mail slots that have been embedded into the wall beside the leftmost apartment.

One of these mailboxes is mine now. Not like I've got anyone to write to me.

Two descending steps to my left reveal a small nook beneath the second flight of stairs and the final door on the first floor.

SUPER is written on the door.

Beneath the staircase itself is a cage, filled with mops and buckets and some dusty Christmas decorations all piled up.

"Let's head up," I say as I turn, my foot catching on a couple of packages at the base of two steps.

I'm falling forward until Derek reaches out an arm to stop me.

"Thanks," I say, feeling my cheeks redden a little.

"Wouldn't want footage of you scattering your teeth across the floor to leak out your first day," Derek says with a grin and a nod to the camera sitting high on the wall above us.

I lift my two suitcases and begin the trek up the stairs.

They're pretty narrow.

I can just tell this place was built pre-war, like a lot of buildings in the city.

On the landing there's a large window, but the glass is frosty so I can't see outside. Not like there's much to see out there anyway, save for more brick. Paint has been liberally applied around the window too, sealing it to the sill beneath the dozens of accumulated layers.

The *landlord special*, as the joke goes. A coat of paint, and everything's fixed.

We continue up the next flight of stairs and finally arrive on the second floor.

I suck in a breath, working to slow my heartbeat.

It's sort of embarrassing how out of shape I am. Two flights of stairs, and I'm already sucking wind.

Derek doesn't seem to be faring all that much better though. Between the weighty suitcase and the heavy cotton work-coat-and-flannel combo he's rocking, he's feeling it too. I can tell from the redness of his face.

He sets down the suitcase with a thud as he reaches the landing and then unzips the faded brown jacket he always wears.

"Warm in here, huh?" he asks.

He's right actually. It's not just how out of shape I am—they've got the heat blasting.

Maybe I've been judging the landlord unfairly.

The place may be a little dingy, but at least they aren't stingy with the heat.

The apartments up here are numbered 3A, 3B, 4A, and 4B, so we've got to keep climbing.

Somehow the staircase seems to get even narrower as I continue up, my arms straining beneath the weight of the suitcases.

Another window at the break, also frosty. With a massive effort I manage to haul the suitcases up the final flight, my chest heaving when I finally make it to the third floor.

"I'm upping what you owe me," Derek says between pants, "to at least two cups of ramen."

"That's fair," I reply.

Footsteps on the stairs from the floor above draw my attention. I glance over at the staircase, finding an older woman slowly descending.

She's draped in a thin purple sweater that doesn't seem nearly heavy enough for the weather today. Considering she looks like she weighs about eighty pounds soaking wet, I can't imagine she's going to be comfortable at all out there.

The hunched woman continues down toward us as we push our suitcases to the side to make room for her.

I swallow and paste a smile onto my face. It's important to be friendly and cordial to neighbors.

"Hello, I'm Salem, I just moved here," I say with my hand raised in greeting as she reaches the base of the stairs.

The old woman's head tilts up to us, her wrinkled face looking between the two of us.

"You shouldn't be here," she hisses.

CHAPTER 2

blink, my hand still extended toward the woman, who brushes by us without another word. Her tiny frame disappears around the corner as she continues to shuffle downstairs.

Her words feel like a bee sting, making my heart beat a little faster.

You shouldn't be here.

"Friendly place, too," Derek says with a whistle.

"What did she mean by that?" I ask, swallowing hard.

"Who knows? Maybe she's jealous of your stylish coat and Crocs combo."

I glance down at my Crocs, which are navy blue and stuffed with little shoe charms in nearly every hole. Not the most stylish attire admittedly, but they're comfy, and they're me.

"Yeah, maybe," I say with an eye roll.

Her words continue to roll around in my mind. That was a little off-putting, but I try my best to forget about it. The woman probably has plenty of her own stuff going on.

Whatever. You can't pick your neighbors, as the old saying goes.

At least she's on the floor above, so chances are we won't be seeing much of each other anyway. Still, the harshness of her words sticks with me, even as I try to forget them.

"Five B you said?" Derek asks, his eyes flicking over the bronze plates on each door.

"Yep."

I clear my throat and push the old lady from my thoughts.

There it is—my new apartment. I'm on the left side of the hallway, with one other door right beside me in a similar fashion to the apartments at the end of the hall on the first floor.

Directly across from me are two more apartments, and then the staircase up to my right.

It's definitely not a large building. Cozy is good, right?

I step up to the door to put my key in the lock, my eyes catching on the plastic sign hanging slightly tilted on the stained, faded white wall beside me.

THIS IS YOUR HOME—PLEASE KEEP THIS SPACE CLEAN, it reads.

Another couple seconds, and the door is unlocked, the thick wood slab swinging inward.

"The big reveal," Derek says from behind me, his eyebrows wiggling.

The landlord did send me a couple photos of the interior in our email exchange, but everyone knows how much difference lighting and angle can make when it comes to apartment photos.

Meaning I'm not entirely sure what to expect as I step inside.

The door continues to open inward until it bumps into the wall.

A narrow hallway greets me, the walls blank and sterile. My eyes flick over the space.

The hall opens up into the living room area, and as we

make our way inside, I find myself struggling to keep a smile off my face.

While it's certainly no penthouse suite, it's mine.

An apartment all to myself.

Derek lowers the suitcase down with a grunt in the main room before planting his hands on his hips and doing a spin.

To my right is the kitchen area, complete with a stove, sink, and refrigerator. Cabinets line the wall above, and a small, scratched window behind the counter lets in some light.

Other than a countertop built into the wall to my left, there's a full bed pushed into a corner. That's it for furnishings.

"Seems decent enough, right Sal?"

I turn to him and smile. "It's perfect. Thanks again for finding this, seriously."

Derek flashes another smile.

"I'm glad. I really think this could work—in fact, I'm actually a little jealous. Maybe I should've kept this find to myself," he says mischievously.

"Oh please," I say with an eye roll, "a bachelor pad needs to be in Manhattan. No offense, but I'm not sure you're handsome enough to get women to agree to come all the way out to Williamsburg for you."

Derek wiggles his eyebrows again and shakes his head.

"About that—I've met someone, actually."

Now it's my turn to raise my eyebrows. "Wait, seriously?"

Derek and I have always been single since we've known each other. That was part of what we bonded over in the beginning–always being alone.

I can't help but feel a little betrayed. Still, I manage a thin smile as Derek nods eagerly.

"She's fantastic—you'd love her, Sal. I think she might be *The One*."

"No girlfriend in four years, and now she's *The One*?"

Derek scratches the back of his head sheepishly. "Okay, okay, you're right. Too soon. Maybe I'll wait another week before proposing then."

I roll my eyes as Derek chuckles to himself over his own joke.

"Now all you've gotta do is find yourself a fella, and we can double date," he says as he steps up to the kitchen sink.

He flicks on the water before lowering his head and lapping it up straight from the faucet like a dog.

"You know there's like… a *million* things in the tap water here, right?" I ask.

Derek straightens, his hand running across his mouth as he grins.

"Oh, come on. It's water. If it wasn't safe, they wouldn't let us drink it."

"You have so much faith in the system," I say with a smile of my own as I shake my head.

Derek flashes another smile. "I think legally, I have to be. Me and the MTA guys, we *are* the system. Without us, there's no NYC."

"Fair enough."

Derek claps his hands together with another glance around the small room.

His eyes settle on a key on the counter.

"Ooh, is this for me?"

The apartment's spare key. I've already decided he should be the one to have it, seeing as he's the only person I really know in the city anyway. Besides, he's never given me a reason not to trust him.

"All yours," I say.

He scoops up the key and brings up the large key ring attached to his belt. There have to be a hundred keys on there, so I have no idea how he'll even know which is mine. Derek doesn't seem fazed however. He attaches it before letting the ring drop again with a metallic jangle.

"You all set then?" he asks.

I nod. "Yeah. Thanks again for helping me, for finding this place. I really appreciate it."

"No problem, Sal. I'm just glad it's decent enough for your liking," he says.

He's being polite—I would've slept standing up in a locker, if the rent was cheap enough.

After another wave goodbye, Derek steps out, and the door claps shut behind him. I reach over and turn the lock, hearing the satisfying thunk as it clicks into place.

My eyes travel up the length of the door, falling on the three other deadbolts that have been painted over.

Seems like overkill to me. Then again, you never really know your neighbors, right?

Now that I'm alone in my studio, it's time to get unpacked.

It won't take all that long, considering I have barely anything to my name to begin with.

At least here, I'm by myself. I step over the wood floorboards, their creaks filling my ears as I make my way back down the hallway.

The room is probably about thirteen feet across, and the same wide. Two windows face a brick wall to my right, allowing enough of the fading daylight inside that I don't have to turn on a light.

I step over to them, only to find these have been painted shut, too.

Ugh. I was really hoping to get a little bit of a breeze blowing through here, despite the temperature outside.

I've always done that, even since I was a little girl. Mom, back when she was still alive, would always chew me out for "wasting heat" by letting it slip out through the opening.

Even after getting in trouble though, I'd still leave the window open just a crack.

I press up against the glass, letting my forehead soak up the coolness. It feels like ice against my skin.

Pressed against it like this, I've got a view of a narrow alleyway below, and a sliver of the street up to my right.

A few people pass the crack between the buildings with their shoulders hunched up and heads hunkered down against the wind, hurriedly headed wherever they need to get to.

As I pull myself off the windowpane, my gaze catches on something.

There are marks in the black paint of the windowsill. Kneeling down, I study the small, unsteady lines.

My hand comes up, and I fit my fingers into position, realizing with a start that they're nail scratches.

CHAPTER 3

My breath catches in my throat at the idea.

I blink a little, taking a step back and chewing on my lip as I work to get my heartbeat back under control.

My head races with panicked thoughts, but I need to do what Dr. DeLuca said and just breathe through it.

Sometimes, the best thing to do is let go…

I take a deep breath, feeling my hands shaking before I clasp them together. Maybe someone was just really eager to get a breath of fresh air. Maybe they got tired of having closed windows, after all.

Besides, if someone really was in trouble in this room, they could've easily broken the pane of glass and shouted for help.

I'm pretty far removed from the street, but I'm sure *someone* would be able to hear me yelling, right?

This isn't helping.

I turn away from the window and look for a light switch. I just need to get some light blazing through here to clear my head. It takes a second to find it, but I do, set into the wall on the left side of the room just above the counter.

I flip the switch, and an overhead light buzzes to life, flickering twice before finally holding steady.

With the light blazing down from above, I breathe a little easier. It's plain to see this is just a regular old apartment. Emphasis on the *old*.

It's my head warping things, that's all.

I get to work unpacking to pull myself from my overthinking. One of the first things to come out of the suitcase is my speaker.

I've had this thing for years, and it's one of my favorite possessions. It's cheap and dinged up from the years of heavy usage, but it's an absolute trooper.

I set it up against the windowsill and connect my phone. Moments later, I've got some instrumental jazz drifting out, the notes grounding me as I dive into unpacking again.

Dishware comes out next. There's not a lot of it. Two ceramic plates, a couple bowls, an *I HEART NY* mug, and two sets of silverware are all I've got.

I'm not much of a cook, though I really ought to be considering how much money I could save. Still, not much is easier than tossing a cup of ramen into the microwave for a minute.

Mom always said I'd never be able to settle down if I couldn't figure out how to cook for a man.

Not like her knowing how to cook kept Dad from leaving.

Next out is my clothing rack, a simple snap together affair that's assembled in minutes. Once I get that built, I start pulling out my meager selection of clothes.

I like to tell people I'm a minimalist, because it sounds a whole lot better than saying *I had to choose between eating next week and a new pair of jeans*.

Black skinny jeans, blue skinny jeans. A couple of blouses, my blue dress, and then my pink sweatpants and sweatshirt. A capsule wardrobe, I think they call it. I call it making less than forty grand a year—in a good year.

I toss my socks and underwear onto the little shelf at the bottom of the clothing rack. It looks a little messy, maybe a little trashy, but I don't expect to have many guests over.

Considering I'm going on four years single, and that streak doesn't seem like it'll be broken anytime soon, who cares?

It's my space, I can do what I like.

Next out is my sheets. I've got two sets, gray and slightly-more-gray.

They're cotton I think and have been with me for so long I can't even remember buying them. Still, I can't bring myself to get rid of them. They're at the point now where they're so broken-in they feel like a t-shirt, and if I close my eyes and imagine hard enough, maybe even a warm embrace.

Pull yourself together, Salem. Way, way too sad.

With a grunt, I manage to drag the bed frame from its corner, stiffening a little at the sight of the spiderwebs that are pulled off the wall as I do so.

I know spiders are the good guys and all that, but still. Yucky.

I turn to decide where I'd like the bed to be. Beneath the windows might be nice, that way I could wake up in the morning's glow.

It takes some effort to get the bed into position, but I get it done. Again, I'm more than a little embarrassed at my state of fitness.

Once the sheets are on, I pull out my comforter and lay that on top. Out next are my two lamps, one tall and one smaller.

Both end up on the floor, as there's no table or anything for them.

Finally I pull out my small smart TV, which cost me thirty dollars second hand. I put that on the stand against the wall to my left.

That's everything. I sit down on the corner of my bed and let out a breath.

This is my space now. My domain. I'm trying to get that through my head when a sudden noise jars me, freezing me where I'm sitting.

It's someone screaming. Screaming *loudly*.

CHAPTER 4

My eyelids snap open, and my heart is nearly in my throat as I scramble to my feet.

The scream is coming from next door. Are they okay? Is someone hurt?

I only make it a couple more steps when more sounds follow the scream.

The sound of police sirens, and then theme music so loud it sounds like it's playing from my apartment, not next door.

My shoulders lower as my fear quickly turns to irritation. Whoever is over there is watching some stupid TV show with the volume up so loud I can hear every syllable.

The music continues to pulse, intertwining with the sirens as the theme plays on. I press a hand to the wall, feeling it literally tremble beneath my fingertips.

It's some live cop show. I know that because I hear the narrator mention the setting is Cranston, Rhode Island before some thickly accented cop starts talking about *speedahs*.

I grit my teeth. I can look past some peeling paint and outdated appliances, but a noisy neighbor is where I draw the line.

I wait a few more seconds, trying to get a hold of my breathing as I let Dr. DeLuca's words wash over me.

You can't control what other people do, only your own actions in response…

It's a good message, I guess, but it does little to quell the burning in my chest. How can this person be so inconsiderate?

They *have* to know how loud their TV is. I wouldn't be surprised if the whole block knows it.

As the minutes tick on, it becomes brutally clear whatever idiot is in there isn't going to turn it down. If anything, it almost sounds louder now that the episode is in full swing. Gunshots and shouts echo through my apartment.

I take another breath, shutting my eyes for a second. To my surprise, I realize my fists are balled. I unfurl my hands, noticing how deeply my fingernails were pressed into my palm.

Being quick to anger was Mom, not me. That's not who I want to be.

I let out a rush of air and then take a few steps to the door again. Even in my entry hall, all I can hear is the stupid show next door.

Pulling open my door, I take a step to my left and stand in front of my neighbor's apartment.

My heart is beating a little faster now, though I'm not entirely sure why. I'm not the one in the wrong here—it's whoever must be deaf inside the room. All I'm going to do is ask them politely to turn it down, anyway.

I rap my knuckles against the door, biting my lip as the echo rings out on the small third floor landing.

While I'm waiting for my neighbor to open up, I glance down the staircase to my left. The frosty window is darker now, telling me it's nearly night.

The seconds tick by, but no one shows. I knock again, rapping three times against the wood.

While I'm waiting, I look around and notice another camera on this level as well. It's mounted just below the ceiling and centered on the wall with the plastic sign telling us to clean up.

A little red light tells me the camera is on.

At least the landlord cares about security.

It's a big problem in NYC, having packages swiped. That's what the camera is for, right?

My second knock goes unanswered too, which is ridiculous because obviously *someone* is in there.

My patience is beginning to wear thin. As much as I don't want to make a scene or anything considering I just moved in, this is crazy.

I lean forward and turn my head so that my ear is resting against the wood. The sound somehow seems a little muffled through the wood, the noises of the cop show dulled as I try to hear whether or not whoever lives in the apartment is coming to speak with me.

The sounds of the show overpower everything, making the effort futile. I lean back with a sigh, raising my hand to knock a third time.

This time I thud hard against the door, putting some real emphasis into each blow and leaving my knuckles aching a little as I pull them back.

For a moment my heart pounds—what will they think about that?

The anxiety gives way to irritation again as *still* no one shows up. Whoever is in there is not coming out, no matter what.

Fine. I think back to the super's room below the stairs. Maybe they can help me.

I head down the steps, taking them a couple at a time.

The second floor is quiet as I pass through. Even though it's only like six in the evening, it seems like everyone has settled in for the night.

Briefly I wonder if this place is filled with old people like the judgmental woman Derek and I encountered on the staircase, all of whom go to bed at seven PM.

It's a possibility. Part of me hoped that moving in here would be a catalyst for me to finally break out of my shell. Maybe even make a few friends. Those hopes are quickly becoming dashed.

I make my way down to the first floor then take a sharp left and step down the final two short steps until I'm on the same level as the Super's door.

It's quiet, apart from my knock against the wood. I step back to wait.

Overhead hangs a single, bare lightbulb, its pale glow illuminating me and the cage beneath the stairs. I glance over at it as I wait, my gaze drifting over the various items stuffed haphazardly beneath there. It looks filled to the brim, and I imagine if someone opened it, everything would come tumbling out like something in a cartoon.

In a repeat of the scene upstairs, the seconds tick by without any sort of answer. My foot taps on the dusty tile as I wait.

What is it about this building and people not answering the door?

I lean forward a little, hoping to hear some sounds of shuffling footsteps or something from the guy inside, but there's nothing. Ugh.

Looks like the super won't be any help. I turn away from the door with a sigh, starting my journey up the stairs once again.

As I make my way up the first flight, I hear a door open somewhere below.

Is that the super, finally?

I race back down the steps, only to see a woman stepping out of her room.

"Oh, hello," I start, mustering a smile, "I'm Salem, I just moved in."

The woman, who is probably in her mid-forties, stares blankly at me. She looks tired, worn-down. The dark roots of her hair are plain to see, showing just how long it's been since she had her hair bleached blonde.

I wait for her to introduce herself, or acknowledge my presence besides the stare, but she doesn't.

The seconds tick on, me standing on the first step and the woman in her doorway, her eyes locked on me.

I can feel myself squirm beneath the penetrating gaze, and I'm almost pinned to the spot as the space seems to shrink around us.

Finally, she moves.

Still staring me down, the woman shakes her head slowly back and forth in the most disapproving look I've ever seen.

Then she shuffles down the hallway and steps through a door to the laundry in the basement.

What is going on?

CHAPTER 5

Long after the loud bang of the laundry door, I stand there, the woman's expression still reverberating through my mind.

The way she shook her head was so declarative, like fact. She didn't even know me, and yet she decided after one look I wasn't supposed to be here.

Trudging back up the steps to the third floor, I find myself struggling not to cry. After everything, it's just too much. It feels like everyone here got a memo before I moved in to hate me, and I have no idea why. My stomach feels tight with dread.

I wasn't looking to make friends with everyone. All I really wanted was a simple hello in the hallways, just some small crumb of human interaction to prove I'm still a person.

I've seen it said that New York City, despite being the biggest city in the country, has some of the loneliest people. I know it's true—I'm one of them.

Almost nine million people living here, and I can't seem to get along with *any* of them.

My footsteps echo through the stairwell as I go, and I

swallow hard around the lump in my throat. It's time to come to terms with the fact that this isn't an ideal living situation.

Lousy, loud neighbors, a crumbling building, less-than-stellar amenities.

Briefly I consider just leaving, packing up again and fleeing in the night.

But where would I go? This was literally the only apartment I applied to that accepted me.

After submitting literally hundreds of applications, I'm not really eager to send out more. To keep getting rejections. Juvenile detention and involuntary commitments to mental hospitals don't exactly have landlords begging for me.

Besides, I signed a one-year lease contract. The last thing I need is the police getting involved and my name coming up.

Again.

So as I reach the third floor, and the sound of the booming TV hits my ears again, I suck in a deep breath and simply plod over to my door.

It's better than sleeping on the street, I tell myself.

At least here, I have a bed. A kitchen. My own space.

I crack open my door, and the heavy wood swings slowly inward as a siren howls on the TV next door.

My eyes fix on the light in my room—or rather the lack thereof.

Staring into the darkness of my studio apartment, my pulse quickens. Did I turn off the light when I left the room?

I can't remember. My brain was so focused on the obnoxious noise coming from next door. Surely I did.

Still, I remain firmly planted in the doorway. My thoughts run wild as I stare into the darkness at the end of the narrow hallway. It's fully nighttime now, and the windows in the room don't offer any source of light.

The only visibility comes from the cold light of the hall bulb behind me, illuminating the hallway like a sterile hospital ward.

The radius of its light only extends a few feet into my apartment before it's swallowed whole by the darkness inside. My mind races as I struggle to remember what Dr. DeLuca said.

Anyone could be in there. Did I turn off the light? What if someone is in there waiting for me?

I swallow hard, balling my fists. Enough.

Walk. Take a step, Salem.

I'm walking forward into my apartment, skin practically buzzing from the pounding of my pulse in my ears.

The TV next door continues to throb, the dialogue of the police making the wall tremble beside me as I pad silently forward.

My door shuts behind me with a dull *thunk*, making me jump and whirl around. It's nearly pitch black in here now that the light from the hallway has been cut off.

I scamper another couple steps forward to the bathroom on the right, flinging my arm wildly inside the door to feel for the light switch.

There it is—I flick it on in a hurry, bringing some much-needed light to the room.

It's a harsh white like the hallway bulb, but I don't even care.

It leaks out of the bathroom and reveals the studio in all its shabby glory. Just me in here, a reassuring sight that allows my pulse to slow a little.

I must've turned off the light automatically when I left and forgotten about it.

At least I'd built up good habits.

The bathroom light gives off a little buzzing sound, distant and low like some sort of insect.

I glance into the bathroom, taking in the small pot toilet and sink crammed in beside it. To my immediate left is a tiny shower. The entire space is small enough that I can touch both walls with my arms if I extend them out to the sides.

Stepping inside, I let my breathing slow a little as I catch sight of myself in the mirror above the sink.

My hair is frazzled from a long day of moving.

Errant strands go off in all directions like I'm some type of mad scientist. Maybe *this* is why everyone is treating me like I'm a freak.

Mom would have something to say about my hair, no doubt.

The bags under my eyes look darker than normal, too. I used to be so pretty, so ready to take on the world. I could've done anything.

I let out a sigh and step away from the sight of myself and head back out into the main room.

It's not late, but I'm feeling exhausted. There's little chance I'll actually be able to fall asleep, though. Not while the walls continue to shake and rumble with the sound of the TV next door.

Standing in the center of my room, I chew my lip, trying to decide what to do.

After another moment, I dive into a suitcase and pull out my headphones. With the noise canceling feature, maybe they'll be able to do some good.

I pull them on, the comforting cups fitting snugly around my ears.

Once they're on, the noise level drops to a tolerable background murmur. I spend more time than I should in these things, really.

Even walking the streets, I've almost always got my headphones on. Probably part of the reason I can't find a guy.

With my near permanent scowl and headphones blocking out the world, I can imagine I must look like the most unapproachable girl in the city. If I don't have them on however, I find that the city gets to be… a lot.

So many noises all at once, it's overwhelming. Much better to dull it down.

Looks like I'll be wearing them a lot around here, too.

I pull out my phone and place an order online for groceries to be delivered tomorrow. I could probably venture outside and find some sort of store nearby, but now that I'm back in my room, I'm not sure I want to leave.

My space means safety, relative peace. I don't know if I could bear another interaction with an unfriendly neighbor tonight.

My phone buzzes, jarring me from my thoughts.

A glance down at the screen shows it's a text from Derek.

All moved in?

I smirk and start typing out my response.

Yep, thanks again for ur help.

At least I have Derek to remind me I'm not totally alone and outcast from society.

Even he's found someone to be with, though. And here I am pulling a crushed plastic cup of ramen out of the bottom of my suitcase to heat up for dinner.

Stepping over to the kitchen, I pull open the microwave and recoil.

Ew. Something sticky coats the inside of the thing, a crusty yellow that makes me want to gag.

Cheap rent, I remind myself.

It takes a couple disinfectant wipes and some serious elbow grease to get the microwave cleaned out, but I feel better once I do.

As the ramen cup spins in the microwave, I turn to the oven and give it a once over. I'm no cook, but perhaps I could try my hand at some recipes now that I've got a kitchen all to myself.

To my dismay however, none of the eyes light when I spin the dials. I notice the little LED display for the time in the center is dark, too.

Fantastic.

Something else to mention to the super, if I can ever get

ahold of him. Maybe tomorrow morning I'll stop by before doing a load of laundry.

After dinner, it's back to my bed. There isn't much else to do in the room, so I pull out my laptop and put on a movie.

It's some silly Rom-Com. As much as I hated Mom, I did have her to thank for instilling a love of cheesy escapist movies. If she'd treated me normally, I wouldn't have needed to turn to movies for a sense of normalcy.

Sure, they're formulaic, maybe a little cliche. That's all true, but they're a comfort to me now, a world where I know everything is going to work out okay, no matter what.

Beyond my headphones, I can still hear the distant roar of the TV from next door. I tap the volume button on my laptop to turn up the sound a little louder.

———

I stir awake, my eyelids fluttering open. What time is it?

A glance up at the dark windows beside me tells me it's still sometime in the night. My computer screen is black on my bed.

I pull off my headphones and work my aching jaw. The cups of the headphones are damp with my sweat from passing out with them still on.

A loud crash breaks the silence, making me jerk—but it's the TV again. Somehow, despite the early hour of the morning, my nocturnal neighbor is still watching whatever garbage they've got on.

The headphones go right back on as I close my laptop and turn over, pulling my thin comforter up the length of my body.

The noise is so oppressive it's hard to fall back asleep, but mercifully I finally do.

The next time my eyes open, it's morning. A quick look at my phone tells me it's just after six-thirty.

By some minor miracle, it's quiet next door, too. I'm beginning to think my neighbor really is nocturnal.

Letting out a yawn, I push out from underneath the covers and spin so my feet touch the wood floors. Instantly I regret it as a sharp spear of pain lances through the sole of my right foot.

A splinter, really?

My limp to the bathroom is filled with grumbling as I plop down hard on the toilet and pull up my foot to get a look at the wound.

My head freezes as I catch sight of the bathroom mirror on the medicine cabinet. It's slightly ajar.

Goosebumps rise across my skin as I remain frozen on the toilet, swallowing hard around the lump that has appeared in my throat.

Did I leave it like that last night?

The seconds tick on in silence, just my shaky breathing filling the air. Slowly I get to my feet and pull open the cabinet the rest of the way, my eyes flicking over everything I've put inside on the three wooden shelves.

It all looks the way it did last night. At least, I think it does. Not like I memorized the layout of my cabinet.

Stop it, Sal. Stop overthinking.

I left the cabinet slightly open. I must've.

As I close it again, I make sure to listen for the magnetic click that tells me it's secure before sitting back down on the toilet.

I wait a moment, but nothing happens. The mirror remains closed.

That's it, then. I didn't shut it all the way last night. Probably was too distracted, which isn't new.

As I fish out my toiletries bag from underneath the sink, I find myself glancing up at the mirror every so often, only to see it still shut tight.

I get out my tweezers and manage to remove the splinter. Definitely going to be socks-only indoors from here on out.

With that settled, I yank on my pair of sweats and bundle up my dirty clothes into a pillowcase to bring downstairs to the laundry room.

While I feel a little guilty for thinking it, part of me is eager to do the laundry now so that I have less of a chance of running into one of my neighbors. I'll pass on the judgmental stares this morning, thank you very much.

Swinging the small load of underwear, socks and t-shirts up onto my back, I slip my feet into the trusty Crocs I've had for years. Most of the shoe charms are fall-inspired. The skeleton, pumpkin, and fall leaves are probably my favorites, even though the skeleton one is hanging on by a thread, and I've had to superglue wire on the underside to hold it in place.

I trudge forward and reach for the doorknob but pause as I notice I forgot to engage the deadbolt last night.

Add that to the list of things to remember from here on out.

As I'd hoped, it's quiet as I make my descent to the first floor.

The dim light bulb above the super's door is still on when I step up to it and rap loudly against the wood.

I'm half-expecting to see the icy lady from last night reappear, but she doesn't.

I rack my early-morning mind to remember what I want to talk to the super about. Next door noise, broken oven. Maybe I'll mention the windows, too—I'd really like to get a breeze.

Just like before however, it's quiet. No response at all. After a minute, I knock again.

The crack against the wood seems abnormally loud to my ears in the otherwise painfully quiet building.

I can't even hear the drum of the city from here, I realize with a start. Pretty good insulation for a pre-war walkup.

My second knock is no good, either. Either the super is still asleep, or out altogether. With another sigh, I hike up the pillowcase again and shuffle to the laundry room.

This door is metal, its coating of white paint marred by a few scuffs and scratches that reveal the dull silver beneath.

I grab the handle and twist, grunting a little as I force the door inward.

I'm surprised to find a man already inside. He glances over his shoulder to look at me as I step inside.

He's tall, probably six-foot-three. Gorgeous too, his almond eyes locking with mine as I enter the small room. To complete the tall, dark, and handsome trifecta, he has dark brown, wavy hair that looks rather perfect for six-thirty in the morning.

"Hello," I manage, suddenly extremely conscious of the raging case of bedhead I've got going on. Combined with my eye bags, sloppy outfit, and no makeup, I must look like a real catch.

The man not only doesn't greet me back, he visibly *stiffens* as I speak. Like it's so awful to say hello to me, he has to regain his composure.

I swallow, feeling my cheeks flush with heat though I *really* don't want them to.

"I'm… Salem," I manage to say, though I don't know why. He's clearly not asking.

The guy remains stoic, his expression cold as he looks back at me. For a moment, I think I'm about to hear him join the club and tell me I don't belong here.

"Victor," he says finally, his voice a deep rumble.

Okay, that's a start.

I open my mouth to wish Victor a good morning, when my eyes fall to the clothes he's putting into the washing machine.

Every item is stained red.

CHAPTER 6

ictor

V   I watch as the girl—Salem, unique name—lets her gaze fall to the shirt in my hands.

I look down at it too, realizing just how much blood is really on this stuff.

Her eyes widen and she takes a measured swallow. Almost in real time, I can see the gears moving in her head.

Come up with something. Anything.

"Nosebleed," I say.

It takes her a moment, but finally she nods and gives me a tight smile.

"Hate those."

I stuff the last shirt into the machine and bring the top down with a clang. I can feel Salem's gaze on me still, but I don't turn around as she steps quietly to the other machine.

It's silent between us as I turn the dials and get everything situated.

It's taken me a little while to nail down the simplest process to remove blood from clothes, but I've got it now.

Before applying any sort of stain treatment, make sure to flush the stain with cold running water. Never hot, only cold.

Next, you have to apply an enzymatic stain treatment to the stains. I prefer bleach. Cheap, available everywhere for delivery. No one bats an eye, although I probably order more than the average citizen.

Sometimes, I even need to use a laundry brush to really penetrate and break down the stain. That's what I spent most of last night doing. The next step is to launder the clothes, like I'm doing now. Again, it's cold water on the regular setting.

This is the first round of washing. Usually it takes two full cycles before the stains are fully removed. Last week, there was so much it took four.

Once the laundry is going, I'm out of there without another word to the girl.

Who knows if she bought the nosebleed story. I'm not sure how much of the shirt was showing from her angle, but I'd guess even a cursory glance would reveal just how saturated the shirt was.

At least she didn't ask any more questions. That's the last thing I need.

The laundry door opens with a squeal as I reach the first-floor landing and turn to start up the second set of stairs.

I can hear her footsteps on the stairs behind me, quiet like she doesn't want to draw any attention to herself.

When I reach the second floor, I pause before heading up the next flight of stairs. There's a brief pause on the staircase as Salem stops too.

When I reach the third floor, I cross the short hall and arrive outside my door.

Footsteps behind me. I glance over my shoulder, my eyes meeting Salem's for a moment before she darts her gaze away.

Instead of heading up to the fourth floor, she walks to the room directly opposite me in the hall.

Of course. It would make sense she'd be put in there. She

slips inside without another word, the door coming shut behind her.

My gaze lingers on the other side of the hall for just another moment, the anger rising up inside of me.

My fists are so tight my skin is turning white. I force a breath and get my door open.

Salem must be new here. With any luck, she'll keep to herself and won't ask more questions.

She can't find out what's really going on around here. If she does, there's going to be trouble.

CHAPTER 7

I chew my lip as I sit on my bed, staring blankly at my computer screen.

I'm supposed to be filling out job applications, but my heart just isn't in it. Maybe it's because I've submitted close to a thousand and haven't had so much as an interview to show for it.

Maybe it's Victor, and the shirt he was washing.

He said the blood was from a nosebleed. I'm still trying to decide if I believe that or not.

Then again, what reason would a stranger have to lie?

Maybe he was just embarrassed about cutting himself cooking, or something like that. It did seem like a fair amount of blood, but I caught just a glimpse of the shirt before he tossed it inside.

Somehow, that interaction was the least weird I've had since moving in here. Victor and the bloody shirt.

Of course he's right across the hall from me, too. One of the most attractive men I've ever seen in real life, and he's the apartment across the hall from me.

Though I don't know any more about him than his first name, I can't stop thinking about him. His shoulders were like boulders beneath the henley he wore. It hung beautifully off his tall frame, hugging the side of his pectoral muscles just enough so that I definitely knew they were there.

I wouldn't mind seeing those pecs without clothes on top.

Sal. Get a hold of yourself.

It's becoming clear I'm desperately lonely. Crushing on the hot neighbor is a tired cliche, and yet here I am.

I clear my throat and get back to scrolling through job sites for any posting that would allow someone like me to apply.

No degree, which means entry-level.

You'd think entry positions would be a dime a dozen around here—but no. I've applied in almost every field you can imagine without any luck.

Customer service, cold-calling, restaurant work. I even got turned down by a mattress store, who stated they wanted to go "in a different direction" with their hiring.

Still, I need to eat. My current job is doing data entry for a law firm upstate, but the remote work isn't nearly frequent enough to be considered a full-time position. It's enough to survive on, that's all.

Try as I might to avoid it, my mind drifts back to Victor. He seemed so appalled that I even spoke to him, which was pretty crushing.

Was it the way I looked?

I chew my lip and glance out the window as the light changes on the brick outside my windows. It's cloudy today, I think.

The view from my apartment doesn't really offer a look at the sky.

I find my eyes drawn to the scratches in the paint again and pull myself away before the upsetting thoughts kick up once more. Taking a deep breath, I dig into the applications.

It's a few more hours before my head comes up again. My eyes ache from staring at the screen for so long, my back hunched in a position that would have chiropractors salivating.

I slide the hot laptop off my thighs and stagger off the bed. It's five in the afternoon now–I've gone through a whole day doing essentially nothing.

The light against the brick is orange and seems to be growing weaker by the second. Soon enough it'll be dark again, and I haven't even gone outside today.

I straighten up with effort, wincing a little as my back voices its displeasure at the sudden burst of movement.

Derek is probably running around with his girlfriend. I wonder if Victor has a girlfriend.

Enough.

My shuffle to the fridge is rewarded with a cold drink from the filtered water container I've got in there. It trickles down through my chest wonderfully, leaving me standing in total bliss with my eyes shut.

Laughter snaps my eyes back open. It's coming from the stairwell, echoing off the walls.

Before I even know what I'm doing, I'm scurrying down my hallway and coming to a stop in front of the peephole.

The tiny opening allows me a view of the entire landing, where I see a girl with beautiful blonde hair that cascades down her back and shoulders throwing her head back as she laughs.

She's on the phone with someone as she reaches the top step, looking like she doesn't have a care in the world.

The pang of jealousy at how perfect her skin is surprises me. I don't necessarily have bad skin, but hers is just so nice it makes me instantly self-conscious of my own.

"Exactly, exactly," she says, still smiling.

Her teeth are so white and straight.

She's holding some coffee in the crook of her arm, an expensive leather purse in the other.

"Okay, I'm at his place. Let me call you back," she says into the phone before hanging up.

She chuckles again and then steps up to Victor's door.

My chest tightens. Of course.

Victor has a girlfriend, and she's utterly stunning.

She knocks on the door, and it opens a second later.

Victor's tall figure fills the doorframe, making my heart quicken a little even as I watch him embrace his girlfriend.

They look so perfect together. So happy.

"Hey Claire," he says, the words rolling out smooth like velvet.

His eyes are locked on her, only her.

She cranes her neck to look up at him, her blonde hair cascading down her back. Victor bends his head and kisses her, their bodies interlocking right in front of me. I can't pry myself away, even though I know I should.

He pulls her inside, and Claire lets out a little shriek before she breaks out into giggles as the door comes closed.

I'm still staring through the peephole, but it's quiet out there now.

I try to tell myself that's why Victor seemed so cold to me this morning. It's not because I'm hideous or anything, it's because he's got a girl, and some random woman he didn't even know was trying to chat him up.

That's got to be it. I fight back against the gnawing envy of Claire in my gut as I shuffle back into the darkness of my apartment, my Crocs catching on rough patches on the floorboards.

I'm alone. Sometimes, I feel like the only person in this city who's still single.

I pull out my phone and fire off a text to Derek almost without thinking.

I might be the most anonymous person in this whole city.

We always complain to each other. Probably not the

healthiest habit, but we agreed venting it out is better than just *stewing in the ew.*

To my surprise, Derek's reply comes within minutes.

You're telling me this like it's news.

I smirk, shaking my head.

Gee, thanks. How's married life treating you?

It takes only a couple seconds for his response to come through.

She's busy tonight, but I'm not—down for HH? I get off in 2 hours.

HH—Horror Hang. A term we coined that makes watching some crappy horror movie and pigging out on snacks seem much more official than it really is.

I fire off a *yes* instantly. As much as I consider myself an introvert, there are times when I don't feel like being alone. Today is one of those days.

A scream from next door nearly knocks the phone out of my hands. I whip my head to the right, only to hear the sound of gunshots that give way to theme music as the stupid cop show starts up again.

It's like clockwork with this guy.

Once darkness falls, the TV goes on. It's all I can do to put my phone back into my pocket and let out a shaky breath.

I'm not putting up with this. Seems like everyone here already hates me, so who cares if I make my next-door neighbor irritated?

This time, I'm not taking no for an answer.

Sirens accompany me as I wrench open my door and step out into the hall, teeth gritted.

My fist comes down against the door, thudding heavily. Once, twice, three times.

Just from the impact alone, I know whoever's in there can tell that I'm pissed.

I wait with my hands pressed into my sides as the seconds tick on.

Are you kidding me?

No answer. I pound again, half-hoping maybe Victor comes out to see what all the commotion is about. Then I remember his perfect girlfriend and think better of it.

Another round of knocking, but the TV volume doesn't lower, and the guy doesn't show himself.

"Hello? Can you *please* turn it down?" I finally say through the door, my heart leaping into my throat at my boldness.

With the volume as loud as it is, there's not much chance they heard me.

No response. It takes me another full minute of stewing in the hallway before I realize I look kind of ridiculous standing out here, steam coming out my ears. The guy isn't showing himself. I march downstairs, headed for the super's door.

If this goes on for another night, I'm going to lose my mind.

Just as before however, there's no answer at the super's apartment either. I'm starting to think someone just painted the word *SUPER* on a broom closet as a prank.

I let out a huff. Now I get why there was no issue giving me this room. I shut my eyes, my balled fist coming up to massage my forehead as I stand beneath the dim light bulb in front of the super's door.

The rent is cheap for a reason. Taking a deep breath, I trudge back up the stairs toward my apartment.

I can hear the noise emanating from the neighbor's place as soon as I hit the second floor.

How is no one else bothered? Has no one else complained?

I must be in the perfect position to hear every syllable since we share what has to be a wafer-thin wall.

Two hours later, Derek texts to let me know he's on the way. He's picking up the snacks, even though I should be the one buying, not him. I don't know how we're going to be able to watch a movie, as the TV next door pretty much overpowers everything in here.

Subtitles it is.

I'm going a little nuts involuntarily listening to my neighbor's show, so I decide to just wait outside for Derek to arrive so we can walk in together. It'll be good to feel some fresh air on my face, even if it is a little breezy.

Pulling on my trench coat, I cinch the waist belt and put on a thick pair of cozy socks before slipping into my Crocs. I've still got my sweats on, but I don't care.

I make sure to slip my keys into my pocket and step outside my apartment, locking it.

Even though I'll only be outside a few minutes, I still can't shake that horrible feeling from last night when I came back inside to the dark apartment.

It doesn't take me long to get down the stairs, and then I'm in the first-floor hallway walking toward the front door.

I pull open the swing door, my muscles burning a little at the surprising heaviness of it.

When I reach the front door however, it doesn't budge.

It's locked.

Not to prevent people from getting in—*but to prevent people from getting out.*

CHAPTER 8

nough, Sal.

Even as I think it, the admonition is not enough to stop the racing thoughts that are beginning to pile up.

My fingers are damp with sweat as I grip the bronze handle.

I tug again, but it's like trying to pull a rock in half.

My pulse quickens, even as I try to calm myself.

I spin around, locating another camera in the corner above me. Its beady eye stares down at me, unblinking.

I take a short breath, working hard to get myself under control. I can't actually be locked in here, there's probably just a malfunction with the door.

That's it. It's old, the whole block is. Maybe the—

A pounding on the glass has me shrieking.

I whirl around, hands shaking as I bring them up to shield myself.

Only it's Derek, and now he's laughing at me.

"I got you good," he says, his voice a little muffled as it comes through the glass.

I let out a shaky breath, my hands coming down as I blink back the tears that have built in the corners of my eyes.

Derek raises his arms, showing the black plastic bags in his hands. "You gonna let me in? I want to forget what the word *calories* means already."

I give a small nod, wrapping my fingers around the door handle once more. This time when I yank, it pulls open easily.

Derek slips indoors a moment later, the bustle of thick fabric filling the tiny space as he works his way inside with his bags.

"Took you long enough. Any longer you might as well have kept me out as a Christmas decoration."

I smile weakly, my hand still on the door. I'm almost afraid if I let go, that somehow it'll get stuck again.

Derek notices my apprehension. "What's up? You look kinda rattled. More so than usual."

"It's nothing," I manage, letting go of the door. "Just… the door seemed like it had me locked in for a minute."

Derek turns back and tries the handle himself, only getting a couple fingers around the bronze as the others are bogged down by the bags.

It comes open easily. He pulls it open and shut a couple more times, his eyes scanning the corners before he nods.

"It seems fine now. Maybe it just needs a little WD-40 on the hinges."

"Yeah, probably."

The door swings closed again with a slow hiss. I watch it close for another second before shaking myself and following Derek, who is already through the second door and standing in the hallway.

"How was your first night?" he asks.

I chew my lip. "About that."

Derek's eyebrow pops up as we head to the stairs.

"This'll be good. What happened?"

I nudge my chin up the stairs.

"You'll find out in a couple seconds."

He looks at me inquisitively but says nothing. We get to the second floor, and already I can hear the TV. It only gets louder as we continue up the steps.

Derek looks around. "That's pretty loud, huh?"

I nod. "It went on all night."

We get to the third floor, where the noise is practically deafening. Derek zeroes in on the apartment beside mine as the culprit.

"Have you asked them to turn it down?"

The withering stare he gets from me in return answers the question.

"I'd complain if I were you. No way I'd put up with that," he says.

"Believe me, I've tried. I have yet to meet the building super."

Derek shakes his head as he nudges at me to open my door.

"There's gotta be somewhere online to complain, right? Like some rental portal or something?"

I unlock my door and open it for him, allowing him and the crinkling bags to pass by.

"I guess I've got the landlord's email, I can try that," I say, shutting my door.

It's a decent idea. Still, part of me feels a tug of apprehension. I'm not sure why—maybe I don't want to cause trouble?

As annoying as the TV is, part of me is a little terrified that the landlord might think I'm ungrateful or something and evict me right away.

Too picky, Salem. Always causing trouble. No wonder they don't like you.

Mom's words.

Once the door is shut and deadbolted, I follow after Derek, who's already in the kitchen unloading whatever sugary junk he's purchased.

"I went with the pumpkin candy corn tonight," he says as he lifts up a bag of candy.

"And for the main course?"

Derek flashes a smile. "The finest oven-baked pizza ten dollars can buy."

My expression tells him the truth even before my mouth can. He whirls around and stares down at the oven.

"You're kidding. This thing is broken too?"

I nod.

"Sal, you've *got* to say something," Derek says as he turns back around.

"I will," I reply, though there isn't much emphasis behind my words.

Derek flips over the pizza box and scans the backside. "Okay, I think we can do this in the microwave, too. We'll just have to cut it in half or something."

As he gets to work performing pizza surgery, I hear a door open in the hallway, followed by more laughter.

Without another word to Derek I'm headed for my door, seeking out the peephole like I'm a junkie and it's my next hit.

Claire stands in the doorway again, Victor blocking the rest with his body.

He's saying something to her, and she lets out another little laugh that sounds so cute and perfect it can't possibly be real.

Claire reaches up and touches the tip of Victor's nose before wrapping a hand around his neck and tugging him down toward her again.

I really should look away and give the happy couple their privacy, but I don't.

"Sal?"

I don't respond to Derek's call from the kitchen behind me.

"What are you doing?"

Claire and Victor separate with a few more giggles. Then

she's stepping away from him, her dainty hand trailing down his wide bicep before she steps lightly across the tile to the stairs.

Victor gives a final wave to her before slipping back inside his apartment and shutting the door.

My stomach churns a little as the sound of Claire's footsteps fades away. She's gone, but my jealousy remains.

I know I shouldn't be jealous of this random, picture-perfect couple. It just hurts knowing that some people are in relationships like that, while I'm stuck alone in a room where the oven doesn't work and the floors give me splinters.

Claire and Victor are like something out of a Hollywood script. I guess I am too, only it's no Rom-Com story like theirs —it's some sad, Oscar-bait tearjerker where the main character gets kicked down time and time again until the movie ends.

I turn away from the peephole and head back into the main room, where Derek is standing with his arms crossed and a smirk on his face.

"Doing a little checkup on the neighbors, were we?"

He's joking, but I don't really feel like laughing right now. To Derek's credit, he can tell, and his expression softens a little.

"What's wrong?"

I shake my head even before speaking. "Nothing. It's stupid. It just… it feels like everyone has someone but me."

My eyes shift up to him. "Am I that ugly and repulsive? I mean, even *you* have a girlfriend now."

"No offense," I add quickly.

Derek snorts. "Right. So you're saying you're lonely, is that it?"

I bite my lip. "Sorta. I guess."

Derek's eyes wash over me, and his gaze feels penetrating for a moment as we both stand there in the kitchen.

"You don't have to be," he says in a low voice, keeping his eyes on me.

My brow furrows. What does he mean by that?

Suddenly, the atmosphere in my apartment has changed. There's a feeling in the air that wasn't there just a few seconds before.

Is he… hitting on me?

"What do you mean?" I ask.

"There's things we could do—as friends—that would make you feel less lonely."

Judging from his tone, it's obvious what he's implying. My eyes nearly pop out of my head at the thought.

"Uh, what? You've got a girlfriend, Derek," I say, more than a little confused.

Suddenly Derek's face lightens. "I'm just kidding, Sal. Geez, where's your sense of humor tonight?"

He's laughing, so I force out a chuckle too. As he turns back to the pizza halves though, I'm not entirely convinced he was kidding at all.

Maybe Derek isn't the guy I thought he was.

CHAPTER 9

We end up watching some cheesy horror flick at nearly full volume to drown out the noise from next door, but I'm hardly paying attention.

I still can't shake the odd feeling Derek's suggestion has given me. The way he looked at me in the kitchen was not how he's ever looked at me before.

Usually we watch a couple movies, but after the first ended, I just told Derek I was feeling kind of tired and ready for bed.

He's gone now, leaving me alone in my apartment with my thoughts.

Maybe Derek isn't the happy-go-lucky guy I originally thought he was. Even though we've known each other almost four years, this is the first time I've seen this from him, and it was honestly a little alarming.

As a woman, I know when a guy wants me or not. I just do.

And as much as Derek might say he was only joking, there was a look in his eye that told me he wasn't. Not entirely, at least.

I turn over in my bed and pull the thin comforter over my

shoulder, adjusting my head position so the pressure against my headphones isn't as severe.

Outside them, the neighbor's TV drones on and on. Tonight though, I'm almost grateful to have something to focus on other than all the thoughts that continue to pile up inside my head.

Derek's weird behavior is one thing, but that's not all I'm thinking about. I can still feel the cool brass handle of the front door in my fingers as I tugged on it and it wouldn't budge.

Locked. Sealed, trapping me inside.

Just like when I was young.

Hopefully whatever malfunction the old door has will be fixed soon.

I'm not a kid anymore, so it's kind of disappointing that the front door not opening for a minute has me so freaked out. I thought I was past all that.

This isn't a horror movie, after all. It's New York City. Old buildings mean more than a few pains.

My thoughts swirl as I think back to Mom and see her shadow in the hallway beneath my bedroom door.

You've been a bad girl, Salem. Bad girls go in time out.

I can still hear the creak of the floorboards as she steps away from my dark room despite my cries.

Soon enough I learned that no amount of tantrums would make her unlock my door.

I shiver, despite being almost ten years removed from all that now.

I'm not a bad girl—not anymore. I've done everything right, I tell myself.

Sleep takes a while to come, but eventually I manage to drift into an uneasy slumber filled with shadows moving behind locked doors.

————

The next day goes very much the same as the day before. Applying for every job I can find, ramen and some cold deli meat for lunch at one. It's quiet next door, as usual. By this point I know it's just the calm before the storm.

Something tells me once the sun begins to set, the vampire next door will begin the routine again. That means I've got to get as much work done as I can before then while I'm still able to focus.

I've got some data entry to do for the law firm as well, and I knock that out in a couple hours of mindless keyboard tapping.

Before I know it, it's nearly three PM. Another day practically over.

Laughter fills the hallway, snapping my head up. My computer lands with a muffled thump on my sheets as I stuff my feet into my Crocs and race for the peephole.

I don't know why I'm so nosy, or why I feel almost compelled to watch Victor and Claire interact.

Maybe it's got something to do with why I love to watch rom-coms so much. Seeing a perfect relationship allows me to live vicariously through it.

I can hear their voices as they come up the stairs together, the two of them talking in jovial tones as if there isn't a care in the world. I'm careful to avoid stepping too hard on the old floorboards, as the creaking that would cause would probably give me away.

Sliding up against the peephole, I hurriedly get myself into position, and part of my mind shouts at the rest of me how pitiful this is. A grown woman whose life revolves around her neighbors coming and going from their apartment.

It's still not enough to turn me away. I shift a little so I can see the top stair, waiting for Victor and Claire to come into view.

I picture the couple in my mind, their bodies brushing up against each other as they hold hands.

Victor's tall frame crests the top of the stairs first, his dark wavy hair catching my eye instantly.

Only once he crosses my field of vision do I realize the girl he's holding hands with isn't Claire.

It's some other girl entirely.

CHAPTER 10

I can't pull myself away.

Victor and the girl are headed toward his apartment door. He's got his arm slung around her shoulder now, his hand hanging down as he gestures while he speaks.

"—didn't even know it," he finishes.

The girl laughs.

She's got bright red hair and wears a black jacket with faux fur around the hood.

Her left hand comes up to touch Victor's back in a way that tells me these two are very comfortable with each other.

My throat is dry. I don't know what to think.

Victor takes only a second to get his keys out and unlock the door. He and the girl slip inside a moment later.

The door closes with a heavy thud, leaving me staring at nothing but the tilted brass lettering on the outside.

I blink.

Did I really just see what I thought I saw? Is Victor cheating on Claire?

For some reason, I'm deeply affected—no doubt far more than I should be. These are two random people I've known for only a couple days of my entire life. I've spoken to only one of them. Once.

And yet, my chest aches a little as I think of Victor's arm draped over the new girl's shoulder, the sleeve of his black shirt catching a couple stray red hairs.

Should I tell Claire?

I dismiss that thought almost as soon as it crops up in my mind.

What would I even say to her?

I don't know her at all, or really anything about her relationship. Maybe it's open, or something. Or the red-headed girl is just a friend of Victor's.

It's not like they were making out the way Claire and Victor did in the doorway or anything. Maybe it's even his sister.

I push away from the door.

That's what I get for sticking my nose in other people's business—a bunch of feelings related to events that don't even concern me.

What I should be doing is focusing on my own life instead of trying to live through others. I reach for my phone, intending to text Derek.

My finger hovers over the keypad, but I don't type anything. His odd suggestion last night still has me feeling strange.

Having exhausted my brain and wrists for the day, I flick on the TV and toss on a rom-com that I know to serve as background noise.

Maybe I should go out for a walk, or something. It feels like it's been days since the sun has touched my skin.

I glance over at the windows to my right, noting how weak the sunlight appears. It's probably pretty cold out there. Maybe I'll just order food and stay in.

It's the easier option. No one to judge me or think what a failure I am.

I pull out a blanket and lay it across the wood in front of my bed, using the frame as a sort of backrest. Grabbing my pillows off the bed, I make a nice little spot to sit and watch TV.

My stomach rumbles. Clearly, the one cup of ramen is not going to hold me today. A quick glance at my bank account sets the parameters for what I'll be able to spend.

I place the order, getting some Pad Thai from the cheapest place that'll deliver. It's a thirty-minute wait, so I settle in and start paying attention to the movie.

Once the time is up, I'm back on my feet and pulling a sweatshirt over my head in preparation to meet the delivery guy at the front of the building.

I've still got my Crocs on, but whatever. Not like it's a fashion show.

I pull my door closed behind me, absentmindedly tapping my pocket to make sure I've got my keys even though I didn't lock the door.

With a door this old, who knows if the deadbolt might slide into place accidentally. I already know the super won't help me if I get locked out. Racing down the stairs, I glance at my phone for updates from the delivery driver.

He's outside and waiting.

I hit the first floor and move quickly down the hall to the front door. I can see the guy through the door, a neon yellow bike helmet propped atop a beanie as he shuffles from side to side in the chilly air.

I pull open the first door, and then approach the second. My pulse quickens as my fingers wrap around the cool brass.

It comes open without effort, allowing me to breathe a little easier. The blast of wind that rushes inside surprises me, making me gasp a little. The delivery guy says my name, and I nod, my teeth chattering as I take the Pad Thai from him with a *thanks* before letting the door slam shut.

The delivery guy is already racing back to his motorized

bike, no doubt off to make another trip to feed another lazy person somewhere nearby.

I begin the journey back down the hallway toward the staircase, only to hear the front door being pulled open behind me.

It takes only a glance to determine who is coming in, based on height alone.

It's Victor. I guess I had the movie playing loud enough that I didn't hear him and the girl leave the apartment.

Only he's alone now.

And as he pushes the heavy door inward, I realize his shirt is stained red with blood.

CHAPTER 11

ictor

It's freezing outside, which made what I just had to do even more of a chore. I shrug off my jacket as I push inside the front door.

I'm not alone.

That girl Salem is standing in the main hallway, staring at me.

I glance down at my shirt and realize why. My shirt has splotches of blood across the front of it.

I should've buttoned up my jacket, but I wasn't expecting to see anyone.

Salem still hasn't moved from her spot against the wall. She's holding a plastic bag, maybe takeout.

She shouldn't be here. She wasn't supposed to see this. I glance up at the camera in the corner and pull my jacket back on before buttoning it up.

I push the second door and join Salem in the hallway. The wide-eyed stare she's giving me is not good.

"Another nosebleed," I say, our eyes meeting.

Salem nods. I watch as her throat twitches with a heavy swallow. She's obviously uncomfortable.

Why didn't I just button up the jacket? I'm not used to prying eyes.

There's no doubt she has questions–they're written all over her face.

Don't ask them.

If she inquires about the stains, there will be trouble.

It's almost a relief when she suddenly turns away and scurries back toward the stairs, clutching her plastic bag between her arms like a child would a teddy bear after a nightmare.

I know something about nightmares.

I remain in the hallway. My jaw is clenched, and slowly I allow it to soften.

This is not good.

I strip off my jacket again and pull my blood-soaked t-shirt overhead. Balling it between my hands, I stalk toward the laundry room.

All I can do is hope she bought the nosebleed lie. If she didn't and tries to look into things further…

She will be dealt with.

That's just the way it'll have to be, and there's nothing I can do to stop it.

CHAPTER 12

I shut my door and throw the deadbolt lock with a trembling hand.

Something is definitely going on with Victor.

One nosebleed story, I can buy. What I just saw however, that was no nosebleed. Not at all.

There wasn't even any blood on his face. Most of the stains were toward the bottom of his shirt, like he'd been standing over whatever had been cut open.

My stomach churns, a mix of tight anxiety and nervousness washing over me in waves. I take a shaky breath and head into my room.

As I set my Pad Thai down on the counter, I hear a quiet click from outside as Victor's door closes.

I lean against the counter and shut my eyes tight, working to regulate my breathing. It's vital that I manage my thoughts before they overwhelm me completely. Somewhere in my brain, Dr. DeLuca's words echo, but they are tiny and weak.

Victor was covered in blood. Again. He saw me see him.

He knows I know.

I swallow around the massive lump in my throat. I can't just sit by wondering, catastrophizing. I need to know.

Racing over to my bed, I flip open my laptop and tap my foot impatiently as the ancient piece of technology begins its slow start up.

It sounds like a jet taking off, but the noise is dwarfed only seconds later as the nightly noise torture begins next door.

I barely even jerk at the sudden scream as it breaks through the air before the theme music plays.

I'm too focused on the task at hand. While working data entry is no dream job—I do it for a law firm. That means I know where to look for information about a person.

Especially information related to crimes that may have been committed.

Finally my computer starts up, and I can log in. I tap in my password and then navigate to my law firm's login portal.

They pay for a few different services that can pull information on people, services that the average citizen might not even know about.

I click over to a tab for looking up criminal histories, only to pause.

I don't know Victor's last name.

My mind racing, I bite my lip as I try to figure out what to do next.

An idea hits me. A dangerous idea. Something I swore I'd never do again.

I'm not a bad girl anymore.

My eyes shift down to my trembling hands as I rub them down the length of my sweatpants. I need to know. If something is going on, I need to know.

Taking another breath, I go to a drawer in the kitchen and pull out a small paperclip.

I slip it into the pocket of my sweatshirt and then move as quietly as possible toward the door, taking care to avoid the noisiest of the floorboards.

My fingers push the deadbolt back while my other hand

grasps the dented doorknob. I twist it as silently as possible, holding my breath as I remain glued to the peephole.

The slightly distorted view shows the dimly lit hallway is empty. The door opens with a small whine, freezing me.

I expect Victor to rip open his door at any moment, eyes wild and shirt soaked in blood.

It doesn't happen.

Wordlessly, I slip into the hallway, bracing my heavy wooden door with the back of my hand so it shuts quietly.

It comes fully closed with another click. Then I'm descending the stairs, my Crocs making little noise as I race to the first floor.

I haven't done this in years. I made a promise I wouldn't.

Today, however, I have to break that promise.

I can hear Mom's voice in my head, scolding me. I can see her penetrating glare and feel that sickening twist in my gut that told me I wouldn't be eating for a couple days.

I'm sweating beneath my hooded sweatshirt. It makes my skin feel hot, itchy, overwhelmed.

Too late now, I'm already on the first floor.

I spin and turn to the line of mailboxes built into the wall beside the super's door.

The weak bulb overhead provides enough light for my eyes to scan the scratched boxes in search of 6B.

There it is. I reach into my pocket and pull out the paper clip, unfolding it as my blood pounds in my ears.

Bad girl, Sal.

Once it's bent the way I need, I stuff the end of the paper clip into the small keyhole on Victor's mailbox.

A quick glance behind me tells me I'm alone on the first floor. It's quiet, absolutely silent besides the clatter of my lockpick in the mailbox keyhole.

I have it open within a minute, my breath catching in my throat as the small door suddenly springs open.

Victor has two pieces of mail.

I grab hold of one, my eyes drawn to the corner of it.

Victor Popov.

Hurriedly I stuff the letter back into the mailbox and close it, my heart pounding.

Wrenching my paperclip from the keyhole, I pull away from the mailbox and start back up the stairs.

No one saw me.

I got what I wanted.

As I put my foot up onto the first step, my gaze catches on the camera at the top of the stairs.

It's pointed right at me.

My blood feels like ice in my veins as I remain pinned on the first step, staring right at the camera.

The red light is on. It's recording.

I glance back at the mailboxes beside the stairs.

Are they in the view of the camera?

It's impossible to tell.

It takes everything I have to summon the strength to take another step forward, but I do it. I can practically feel a pair of eyes beating down on my back as I head back up the steps, my mind racing.

What if someone saw me break in?

It's a federal crime to mess with a mailbox. I swallow hard. With my history, that'll be it for me.

No more chances.

I feel lightheaded, swaying a little as I turn and start up the second staircase. I need to hurry back to my room.

I take the second-floor stairs in quick succession, arriving on the third floor within a few seconds. The TV is blaring as usual, covering the sound of my footsteps.

I'm at my door in an instant.

Back inside, I close the door as slowly as possible. My body is absolutely painted with sweat beneath my hoodie. I shut my eyes and lean against the door, my forehead coming down on the old wood.

I risked everything for that. If someone decides to check the footage, not only will I be kicked out of this place, I'll probably end up being taken away in cuffs. *Again.*

I take a shuddering breath.

It has to be worth it.

Shooting back over to my computer, I whisk my finger across the mousepad to get the screen out of sleep mode.

An exasperated sigh slips out as the jet-takeoff procedure begins again.

Once I can log in, I do. I'm back on the law firm's page and typing in the name *Victor Popov.*

I click ENTER.

My heart thuds in my chest, almost loud enough to be heard over the thundering of the television set next door.

It takes a couple seconds for the page to load.

When it finally does, however, I almost wish it hadn't.

Maybe not knowing would've been better.

CHAPTER 13

Victor Popov.

Arrested 09/12/2020 on Assault charges. Charges dropped.

Arrested 03/04/2021 on Assault charges. Charges dropped.

Arrested 10/23/2021 for Strangulation/Criminal Obstruction of Breathing or Circulation. Charges dropped.

I stare at the screen, my chest feeling almost as if it's about to burst. Victor's record is extensive.

There's violence here, real violence. Since New York doesn't have explicit Domestic Violence charges, it looks like he was booked under "Assault." The fact that the charges were dropped tells me the girl didn't wish to pursue legal action.

Devastating, but unfortunately a reality that's all too common with victims of abuse.

The bloodstains on his shirt rise up again in my memory, making me shiver.

Who is my neighbor?

I think again of the girl with the red hair. *I didn't see her leave.*

I swallow hard.

What if something happened to her? What if I was one of the last people to see her alive?

I think about calling the police but think better of it. What do I really know, honestly?

Sure, it's creepy Victor seems to have blood on him almost every time I see him. But for all I know, he's a butcher.

If the cops showed up, they would ask questions. They'd probably pull feed from the multitude of cameras around the place to corroborate my claims.

Then they'd see me breaking into the mailbox, and that would be that.

No cops, then. At least not yet.

I won't sacrifice my future unless I'm sure.

I think of Claire again, her beautiful smile. The way she lovingly touched Victor, running her small hands across his arms. Does she know about his criminal history? Does she know he comes home covered in blood?

She mustn't. Somehow, he's got her convinced. Psychopaths can charm anyone.

As I settle into bed, I can hardly shut my eyes. Part of me thinks if I do, I'll see nothing but blood stains everywhere.

I can hardly breathe beneath the covers. The noise from next door presses in, almost seeming to jeer at me like some laughing phantom as I shrink down beneath the sheets.

I might live across the hall from a horrible, horrible man.

Or maybe I've been alone so long, my brain has started to malfunction. It's impossible to tell what's really going on.

All I know for certain is Victor was dangerous. Whether he still is, remains to be seen.

———

It's morning, but I hardly even notice. Sleep largely escaped me last night, leaving me feeling hollow and brittle.

I stand in the kitchen, hand wrapped around my *I HEART NY* mug that has long since cooled.

Maybe I should go back to bed. My body is screaming for some proper rest, but my mind won't cooperate. I cough a little into the back of my hand.

Am I getting sick?

Probably from the lack of sleep, which is when the body heals.

I'm so out of it, I almost don't hear the noises from the hallway until it's too late.

Suddenly I snap back to attention–laughter in the hallway. Is that Claire?

I set down my mug in a hurry, sliding over the wood boards in my haste to get to the front door.

The sleep deprivation makes itself known as I come down on a couple of the creakier floorboards, sending my heart nearly leaping into my throat.

I come up against the door, hoping the sound of their voices obscured any noise I might've made.

It seems like it has, as Victor's wide back remains turned away from me as he speaks to someone in front of him that I can't see.

He's got his arms out, but with the angle of the door and Victor's size, I can't figure out who it is.

Finally, she moves.

It's *another* new girl. This one has shoulder length brown hair and a septum piercing.

She throws a glance over her shoulder to look back at Victor, grinning widely as he takes a step toward his apartment with her.

My pulse quickens. Another new girl.

First Claire, then the red head, now this girl.

The way these two are touching, there's simply no way they aren't more than friends.

I feel my hands start to shake as I remain glued to the

peephole.

Is Victor simply cheating on Claire?

Or is he doing something much, much worse?

Regardless, Claire needs to know. I have to find a way to tell her what I've seen.

Victor opens his door, and the girl disappears inside. I expect Victor to follow her in, but for some reason, he doesn't.

He's standing in his doorway like he's frozen. Or waiting for something.

One second passes. Another.

What's he doing?

Then Victor begins to turn. It's a slow movement, almost like a mechanical toy being spun around.

His eyes settle on my door. *On me.*

He's crossing the short distance between our apartments before I can even react.

CHAPTER 14

Victor

My fist comes down hard against the wood, shaking the door frame.

My jaw is clenched again. I don't soften it this time.

Salem doesn't open the door—like that's going to fool me.

I heard the floorboards creak as Vanessa and I came up the stairs. Either Salem thinks I'm stupid, or she's got way too much faith in this old wood door.

Two more seconds pass, the silence permeating the hall. She isn't going to open the door. Fine.

"I know you're there," I hiss.

Salem doesn't respond.

Still, I know she's behind the door. There would be a little swishing sound that would've told me if she left. I lean closer to the wood so she can hear every syllable that comes out of my mouth.

"You need to stop watching me," I say, my voice low.

My teeth are gritted, grinding against each other as another second passes.

"Mind your own business, Salem. I promise you, you won't like what happens if you don't."

With that, I turn on my heel and head back toward my apartment. I pull open the door and prop up a smile across my face, though I don't feel like smiling.

Vanessa is in the kitchen area, already necking a beer even though it's barely ten in the morning.

That annoys me, but I try my hardest not to let it show. Annoyance would only interfere with what I have to do.

My door clicks shut behind me, and Vanessa spins around.

"What took you so long?" she asks around the mouth of the beer bottle.

"Just speaking with a neighbor," I say.

Vanessa grins. "That's nice. Is it a real neighborhood vibe here? Everyone knows everyone kinda place?"

I manage a thin smile. "You could say that."

"Your apartment is smaller than I thought it would be," she says as she glances around.

I tilt my head as she laughs.

"Sorry, that was rude. I mean, it's still nice. Want a beer?"

Biting my lip, I shake my head. Each step forward takes effort. It doesn't fill me with pleasure, what I'm about to have to do.

Still, I have to. I have no other choice.

Vanessa shows her back to me as she leans over to peer into the fridge.

"You got something to eat around here? What pairs well with cheap booze?"

Her short brown hair falls in front of her, revealing the skin of her upper back. It's tanned with a few freckles.

I take another step toward her, my mouth going dry.

I really don't want to do this, but I have to.

Vanessa still doesn't turn around.

I tell myself in a few minutes, it'll all be over. I won't have to think about what I've done again, at least until the next time.

And unfortunately, there's always a next time.

CHAPTER 15

'm still shaking.

Victor's words bounce around my head like tennis balls.

Mind your own business. You won't like what happens if you don't.

It wasn't just the words themselves. It was the way he said them.

So matter-of-fact. Not a threat, a declarative statement.

I wring my hands together, my eyes drifting downward as I watch my hands tremble. I cup them together between my legs and try not to burst into tears.

Victor knows I've been watching him. He *knows*.

When he walked across the hall to my door, my mind froze. I couldn't move, even though I should've run.

He would've heard that, though. He knew I was there, he knew I'd be listening.

A chill runs down my spine. I've got to tell someone before all this eats me alive.

I pull out my phone, instinctively tapping on my text exchange with Derek.

My fingers hover only a second before I fire off a text. Yes, things between us feel a little weird, but maybe he really was just kidding. He's always been a jokester since I've known him, and this wouldn't be the first time he's taken a joke too far.

Around tonight?

I could really use a friend. Someone to serve as a sounding board, who could tell me what I should do next.

In a moment of true desperation, I even think about calling Dr. DeLuca but quickly disregard that.

Probably not the best idea to involve my psychiatrist in all this.

I wait by the phone for Derek's response but give up after a couple of minutes. He's at work right now, which means it might be a little while. I'm not sure what to do with myself. I don't have any more work to do for the law firm, and I'm a little afraid to leave the apartment.

What if Victor is out there?

Even though I haven't heard his door open or shut in the past few hours, part of me still wonders if he's sitting in front of my door, just waiting for me to show up.

I hate this feeling. I hate feeling afraid.

Mom made me feel afraid.

I flick on my TV, turning on another cheesy rom-com, the first one I can find. I just need some mindless entertainment to take my mind off of things and to stop myself from spiraling out.

The hours drift by lazily, the afternoon disappearing as I start up a second movie. I'm only half watching, some part of me still primed and ready for any sounds from outside of my apartment.

That's when I hear it.

It's Claire, her voice cutting through the haze in my mind as I whip my head up toward my hallway.

She's coming up toward the apartment. It sounds like she's talking on the phone again.

I slip out of bed in a moment, my throat going dry as I think about what to do.

I feel like I have to tell her what I've seen. I've just got to, right?

Even though we don't know each other, I feel a compulsion to tell her the things that I've seen, girl-to-girl.

The blood, the other women, all of it. I freeze only a couple steps down my hallway as I hear Victor's door open.

For a moment, I wonder when the other girl left.

Then I remember the two movies I watched and realize she must've slipped out during that. If she left at all.

There are so many competing theories rushing through my head, I don't know what to think.

The biggest thing on my mind right now is Claire's safety.

The only thing I do know for sure is that Victor has a history of violence.

I hear his voice as he says something I can't quite understand, my body still frozen a few steps from the door. Any closer, and I risk him knowing that I was listening again.

After our last confrontation, I have a feeling he won't be too pleased if he finds out I'm still snooping.

"Talk to you later, I'm outside. Yeah," Claire says lightly before she hangs up the phone.

It sounds a little muffled coming through the thick wooden door, but it's still clear enough that I can make it out, as the TV next-door hasn't started up yet.

"Hey you," Claire says to Victor.

My heart sinks. I can hear in her voice just how much she likes him.

Victor says something in a voice too low for me to hear clearly, and then his door shuts with a thud, cutting me off from everything.

I swallow hard, finding the shaking in my hands has started up again.

Should I have said something?

What if Claire just walked into the jaws of death, and I stood by and did nothing but watch?

I wring my hands together and pace back into my room as I rack my brain for what to do next.

Should I call the police?

No–that's not the answer.

My TV is still playing, but it might as well be on mute. I can't focus on anything but Claire in Victor's apartment, a lamb to the slaughter.

What if he's doing something to her right now?

What if just a few feet away from me, there's a girl being killed?

I couldn't bear the thought of someone's death being my fault.

The minutes pass in agony, my foot tapping on the old floorboards as I sit as still as possible, trying to listen for any sound from across the hall.

Within another couple of hours, the sun begins to go down. Right on cue, the TV next door flicks on. It's like clockwork.

This time, I don't so much as twitch. I'm expecting it now, and it's the least of my concerns.

The disruption itself isn't a big deal. I'm more worried about not being able to hear Claire and Victor if they leave.

I need to make sure that she leaves.

My hand comes down on the wall, slamming into the chipped paint.

The repeated pounding really couldn't send a clearer message, and yet the volume remains unchanged.

I shake my head. Unbelievable.

At least I know that the noise from next door will mask any sort of creaking sounds on the floorboards as I stride back over to my door.

I spread my legs wide until the outsides of both feet are

pressed against opposite walls to plant myself in front of the peephole.

I'm going to stand here and watch as long as it takes. Until I know that Claire is okay.

There won't be any more sneaking around. I need to see her walk out of there of her own volition, or I will call the police.

The minutes continue to tick on as I stare through the peephole.

My warm breath blows back into my face as it bounces off the wood door I'm pressed up against.

It fogs up the view a little bit, forcing me to pull back for a moment and wipe at the small circle of glass with the corner of my sleeve before putting my eye to it again.

The scene outside hasn't changed. I'm not sure how long it's been, but the hall outside my apartment is the same as ever.

I look out at the two shut doors, which provide no answers as to what's going on behind them. I haven't heard any sort of noise, but that could just be because of the television's volume.

The cop show is in full swing now, and strangely enough I recognize some of the dialogue. I think they've seen this one before.

Great, so they love to watch reruns, too. As if I needed another factor to drive me insane.

My back starts to cramp a little as I remain hunched in front of the peephole, switching eyes every few minutes to give the other one a break.

I straighten myself , wincing a little at the knot in my back that has formed from holding such an uncomfortable position for however long I have been.

As I do, I hear a door swing open.

In a second, I'm back to the peephole, hungrily eyeing

whatever is happening on the other side as my heart rate skyrockets.

A flash of blonde hair in the opposite doorway. Claire's okay.

A wave of relief washes over me as I watch the beautiful girl laugh over her shoulder before pulling the door shut.

She has a glowing smile on her face, looking as if she's the happiest girl in the world.

She must truly have no idea what Victor is capable of.

A plan develops in my head, a wild one.

With the sounds from next door, Victor won't be able to hear my own door open and shut. I can slip out and catch Claire in the hallway to warn her.

She digs her hand in her purse for a moment before pulling out her phone, her face illuminated by the glow of the phone screen as she heads toward the staircase.

She puts one manicured hand on the handrail and begins to step down, her blond curls bobbing with each step.

Just in case Victor is watching, I let the seconds tick by. If I race after her immediately, he might try to stop me.

I need him to feel sure that I'm not going to follow, while still being able to catch Claire downstairs.

Racking my brain, I try to remember how long it takes me to get inside from the front door.

I have maybe thirty seconds total, and that's pushing it.

Each second that passes is marked by the rhythmic pounding in my skull.

I remain glued to the peephole, hearing Claire's footsteps getting quieter and quieter as she heads down the stairwell.

After another ten seconds, I can't stand it any longer. If I continue to wait, I might miss her altogether.

I just have to hope that Victor is no longer watching, if he even was to begin with.

I open my door as quietly as possible, ironically now thankful for all the noise from my neighbor as it completely obscures any sound of me slipping out and shutting my door with a click behind me.

I take the stairs three at a time, practically leaping over them as I hit the bottom of the second-floor landing and start racing down to the first floor. Straining my ears, I can just hear the sound of footsteps from somewhere below.

Claire is still here—I've still got time to catch her.

Picking up the pace even more, I basically throwing myself down the remaining steps to land hard on the first floor.

Unfortunately, I come down weird on my foot, sending a spear of pain spiking through my left ankle as I wince before straightening.

The sudden flurry of motion spins Claire around in the hallway, her face popping up from her phone screen as she looks back toward me.

"Are you okay?" she asks.

I suck in a breath as I look up at her.

Finally, I'm able to manage a nod and take a couple steps toward her, trying to obscure my slight limp as my ankle continues to burn.

"Just tripped a little, that's all."

Claire gives me a smile and begins to turn around, but I can't let her go.

I have to warn her. I have to say something.

"Listen—you're with Victor right?"

That brings Claire's attention away from her phone and back up to me.

She's probably wondering how in the world I know that, so I'm going to have to explain that I've been watching.

"Yes?" Claire says apprehensively.

It's obvious she's a little weirded out. I've approached this all wrong.

I'm flushed, sweaty. I probably look half-insane too, my hair going crazy in all directions.

I look down at my busy Crocs, realizing those aren't helping my case either.

Taking a deep breath, I run my sweaty palms down the length of my sweatshirt to gather myself. It's important I give it straight to Claire as best I can without seeming nonsensical.

"I live across the hall from him, that's how I know," I say quickly.

"Oh. Okay," Claire says.

From the way she's looking at me, I can tell she's definitely uncomfortable.

I raise a hand to her. "What I'm going to say might sound a little weird, but I just need to let you know. Not sure if you're aware, but the couple of times I've run into Victor he's been covered in blood."

Claire's face clouds at my words.

I swallow hard and continue. "Also, I've seen him with a few other girls when you're not here. I just wanted to—"

Claire's face has gone from clouded to angry. It's an odd expression for her beautiful features, her manicured eyebrows pressing together as her lips purse and she tightens her grip on her phone.

"What is this?" she says to me, taking a step back.

"I'm just saying, I think Victor might be dangerous. He's got a record to and–"

Now Claire's putting up a hand and shaking her head.

"Stop talking," she says to me.

"But listen, Claire, I—"

Claire's eyes widen. "How do you know my name?"

"Are you stalking me?" she asks, her voice catching in her throat.

This is not going how I planned at all.

I smear my hands again, raising them up in a gesture of surrender.

It does no good, as Claire is already walking away from

me, throwing her head over her shoulder every few seconds as she looks back toward me with fear in her eyes.

"Please listen to me," I call after her, taking a couple steps forward.

Claire shakes her head.

"You're insane. Leave me alone. Leave me *and* Victor alone."

I open my mouth to try and say something else, but no words come out.

"If you don't I'll… I'll call the cops—I mean it," Claire says, her small voice coming out forcefully as she wrenches open the first door and slips through it.

She gives me another fearful glance before stepping out through the front door, leaving me standing there in the hallway in my Crocs.

That did not go how I planned at all. In my mind, I see Claire outside on the front steps, hurriedly typing out a message to Victor telling him everything I've just said.

My heart pounds with real fury now.

I race back toward the stairs, taking them three at a time as I lunge my way up.

My ankle continues to shriek in pain, but I ignore it as I sprint back up to my room.

I don't want to get caught by Victor away from the safety of my apartment.

I hit the second floor and keep going, pure, primal fear taking over as I imagine his large figure ripping open his door and stepping out to obscure the way.

As I reach the third-floor landing, I'm expecting to see him waiting for me with his massive arms crossed, his shirt splattered with blood as he stares at me.

He's not there.

I stumble toward my apartment, practically tripping over the tile as I rip open my front door and slam it shut, not concerning myself with staying quiet in my haste to get inside.

I throw the deadbolt and only begin to slow my breathing once it's done. I'm safe now.

Leaning against the entry hall wall, I take a moment to catch my breath, shutting my eyes and tilting my head back. My hand comes up and rubs my exhausted face, as I work to pull myself out of my stupor.

I shouldn't have approached Claire like that. Now she thinks I'm stalking her, or maybe she thinks I want her boyfriend for myself.

Either way, it's clear she didn't believe a word I was saying. I probably came off like some mental patient.

There's no doubt she'll tell Victor everything I said, which means if I see him again, there's going to be trouble. His words echo through my mind again.

Mind your own business, you won't like what happens to you if you don't.

I've done exactly the opposite.

I can hardly walk straight, my body is trembling so much as I make my way into the living area.

What is Victor going to do to me?

I'm not sure I'll ever leave my apartment again.

I collapse in a heap on the bed, feeling exhausted and wide awake at the same time. All the events of the past few days are crashing down on me, combined with the adrenaline rushing through me as my mind races unchecked.

I hope I haven't endangered Claire even more.

As I sit there, sobs wrack my chest, coming from deep inside me and surprising me a little.

I grab my comforter and pull it tight, going horizontal until my head is buried in the pillow.

It's dark outside, but it's not late. I can hear the wind battering my windows, shifting the frames ever-so-slightly as it presses into them.

The television next door continues to roar, the booms and crashes coming from the show keeping me on edge. I can't relax, even for a moment.

I grab my headphones and pull them on, but even my music does little to calm my nerves.

I'm worried about Claire.

She's too in love with Victor to see what I see—if there is something to see at all. Maybe Claire is right, maybe I am insane. All of this is maddening.

I dismiss that thought. I *know* I'm not insane… right?

Victor has shown up with bloodstains on multiple occasions, and I know for a fact that he does have a record. That's not something I'm making up. Why couldn't I have explained that better to Claire?

In the moment, all of it rushed out of me in a jumble. I never seem to say what I want to say.

I just have to hope that I'm wrong. The tension in my body is finally beginning to drain when a sudden thumping at my door spikes my heart rate all over again.

CHAPTER 16

freeze, my entire body going still as the thuds hang in the air.

Was that my door?

Between my headphones and the sounds from next door, I can't tell where all the thumping was coming from.

I don't hear it again.

Slowly, I take off my headphones and sit up in the bed, almost unable to swallow with the lump in my throat.

My stomach is tight. I feel nauseous.

Was that Victor? Is he here to do something to me?

I listen again, trying to hear around the blood brushing past my ears. It's tough to make out anything with the oppressive sounds from the television so I slip out of bed and take a couple steps toward the hallway, creeping forward on my tiptoes.

Another thump stops me. It's *definitely* my door.

I glance around the kitchen for a weapon, my eyes falling on a couple of knives.

They're just regular kitchen knives, since I don't do much cooking at all. Even still, I grab hold of one of them, clasping it between my fingers and completely unsure about what happens next.

"Sal?"

My head comes up. That wasn't Victor. That was Derek's voice.

What's he doing here?

I take a few more slow steps forward, almost feeling like this is some sort of trick planned by Victor to lure me out of my hiding place.

I ease up to the peephole and see Derek.

He's leaning against the door, partly obscuring the peephole as his arm comes up again, and I can see a wobble in it.

"Sal, it's me," Derek says, his words coming out a little slurred.

He lets out a giggle as he takes a half-step backwards. He's drunk.

I unlock the door and yank it open.

Derek smiles at me, his gaze catching on the knife in my hand. His arms come up in an *I surrender* gesture.

"Woah, now. Just me."

"What are you doing here?"

His brow furrows. "You texted me earlier asking if I was around," he said, sounding a little confused.

That's right, I did. After all the afternoon activities, I'd completely forgotten about that.

I let out a breath, my heart rate finally beginning to slow as I stand back from the doorway.

"Oh yeah, that's right. Sorry, I'm just a little scrambled."

"Clearly. Who are you planning to stab with that butter knife?"

I hurriedly shut the door behind him and throw the deadbolt again, peering through the peephole a final time to see if there's anyone out there. The hallway's empty.

No sign of Victor.

I let out another huff of air and urge Derek into the main room.

He takes a few hitching steps and claps his hands, rubbing them together as he lets out a shiver.

"Cold out there," he says.

He looks over my apartment. "Love what you've done with the place."

I glance at my phone and see that it's a little after seven. "I wish you'd texted me so I could've gotten some food for us or something," I say as I toss my knife back into the kitchen drawer.

It clatters inside as I slide the drawer shut.

Derek gives me another smile. "Wanted to surprise you."

"I was going to text you asking you to let me in, but then somebody stepped out, and I was able to slip inside," he says.

"Well, feel free to help yourself to some ramen. I think I've got some saltines as well if you really want to gorge yourself," I say, managing a smile.

Derek moves over to the fridge. Each of his steps seems a little shaky. He must really be intoxicated.

"I'd ask how you are, but I'm assuming by the fact you came to the door with a knife, I already know the answer," Derek says.

I can't deny that. Things have not been spectacular, and there isn't any point in lying to him.

"I guess I haven't been so good. There's this guy who lives next door, and…"

I know what I'm about to say sounds a little insane. My next-door neighbor might just be a serial killer.

I picture Derek bursting into laughter at that and steel myself in the event that it happens. Still, I need to get it off my chest, need to share my findings with someone else and get their opinion on it.

Ideally, I'd be able to do that with someone who wasn't grossly inebriated, but I have to take what I can get.

"Well?" Derek asks, his eyebrows pushing up his forehead.

"I think the guy across the hall might… might be dangerous," I finish.

Derek shrugs. "Well that's definitely possible. This is New York, after all. It attracts all types. Has he done something to you?"

"As in tried to hurt me or something?"

I shake my head.

"Not exactly, but here's the thing. I've seen him twice now with blood all over him, even though he told me it was a nosebleed. When I looked him up online, I found that he's got a record of assault, too."

Derek's eyes widen as he scratches his head. I notice he's leaning against the counter for support.

"Oh. Creepy," he says.

I give a small nod. "Yeah."

"Now we know why the rent is so cheap," Derek says with a small smile, trying to keep the conversation light.

Usually I appreciate the humor, but not tonight. I'm trying to address real concerns here, and it doesn't seem like Derek is taking them all that seriously.

I cross my arms, and Derek notices.

"Okay, that wasn't cool. Sorry, I'm kinda drunk. Me and some of the guys had a few after our shift, and…"

He chuckles, then clears his throat.

"So, the guy has a record," he says.

I nod.

"Recent?"

I look away. "The charges were from over three years ago."

"And nothing since?"

I'm quiet for a moment. "No."

Derek chews his lip but doesn't say anything.

"What have you seen him do?" he asks finally.

"I've seen him with a few different girls."

Derek's eyebrows come up again.

"He's getting violent with multiple women?"

I shake my head. "No, not violent. He… I think he's got a few different girlfriends, or something. I don't know."

Derek stares at me another moment with what looks to be almost pity.

"What?" I ask, feeling my cheeks redden.

"I just… I wonder if you've been staying inside too long, Sal," he says quietly.

My brow furrows. "Are you serious? You don't think the guy is dangerous? He's gotten arrested for hurting women," I say, my voice rising.

"And you've got multiple stays in a psych ward," Derek lets out.

I close my mouth, his words feeling like a slap. I can tell from the look on his face he instantly regrets saying it.

He takes a step forward. "Sal—I'm sorry. I'm hammered and acting dumb. All I'm trying to say is maybe you're reading too much into things, that's all."

I bite my lip. He's the only person I've told about Mom having me involuntarily committed to the hospital when I would act up.

I told him that in confidence, and he's using it as cannon fodder against me like I'm actually insane or something.

Despite the sting of his words, there might be a kernel of truth there, too. Maybe I really am reading too much into things.

Victor definitely has something going on, but there's no concrete proof that it's illegal, whatever it is. After all, cheating isn't against the law.

Maybe he's just mad at me because I'm consistently in his business, and revealing to his girlfriend what he's doing behind her back.

"So what do you want to do? Have you called the cops?" Derek asks.

I shake my head.

"Like you said, no proof," I answer quietly.

That, and I had to illegally break into his mailbox to figure out his last name.

I don't tell Derek that part. The less people know about that, the better. Especially with Derek's apparently rather loose lips when it comes to my secrets.

Derek gives a slow nod of his head.

He's still looking at me with a mix of worry and pity that makes my stomach churn.

"Maybe you should get out of the city for a few days. We could take a trip, maybe. Go hiking in the Catskills, or something."

"I'll be okay," I manage, but I don't sound so convincing.

Another thought hits me, and I glance up at Derek.

"What about your girlfriend? Not sure she'd take too kindly to us galavanting off to the mountains together."

I expect him to laugh, but he doesn't. Instead, his eyes are focused on me intently as he crosses his arms.

"Why do you always bring her up? Is it because of her that you don't want to do anything with me?"

His words come out sharp. I blink, completely taken aback by the turn in the conversation.

Derek takes a step forward, nodding. "I'll break up with her if that's the case. Then it can be just you and me."

All of a sudden, the walls of the apartment feel even closer. It's like all of the air has been sucked out of the room, leaving Derek and me alone in nothingness.

I can smell the booze on his breath as he continues to look at me.

There's a hunger in his eyes that sends a chill through me. Derek is most definitely *not* joking.

I take a step back, wanting to put some space between us.

"It—it has nothing to do with your girlfriend, Derek. I just… I don't see you that way."

I hope the words placate him, but they seem to have the opposite effect. He licks his lips, his eyes narrowing slightly.

"You owe me, you know," he says in a low voice.

It comes out slowly, each word hanging in the air as my blood runs cold.

CHAPTER 17

"Owe you? Owe you for what? The food?" I ask incredulously, a strangled laugh escaping my throat.

Derek shakes his head, his eyes never leaving my face.

"For finding this apartment for you. For being there when no one else was. I even helped you move, to show what a kind guy I am. I should get something in return," he says.

This is insane. Drunk or not, I've never seen Derek acting like this. I cross my arms in front of my chest, conscious of how much I'm trembling.

I hope it doesn't show.

"I'd like you to leave," I say.

Derek remains leaning against the counter, the smell of alcohol emanating out of his pores. For a second, I don't think he's going to listen to me.

Finally he gives a brisk nod, and then pushes off the counter.

He adjusts his jacket and then jams a finger in my face.

"Fine. *Fine*, Salem. I'll leave, because I'm a good guy. You'll regret not seeing that."

Then he turns and marches toward my front door without

another word. He rips it open and steps out, breathing heavily.

Then the door clicks shut, and I finally allow myself to breathe.

Now it's my turn to slump against the counter, the fight having been completely sucked out of me. I manage to make my way to the door and engage the deadbolt again with a quick look through the peephole as I do. No one is out there.

What a day.

I don't know what to think now. Am I completely over-reacting?

It seems like everyone I know thinks I'm nuts.

Derek's words still sting, but that's one part of today I don't have any regrets about. Making him leave was the right decision.

Derek isn't the guy I thought he was.

Still, part of me continues to wonder if there are any grains of truth to his argument. I don't have any proof of anything, save for Victor being a skeezeball.

In fact, it's quite possible that between the two of us, I'm the only one who's committed a crime recently. All of it is so confusing. It doesn't help that I'm exhausted.

The reason for my tiredness lets off another loud bang, jarring me. Sounds like they're watching some ghost hunting show or something, judging by the screams every couple of seconds.

I reach into the fridge to pull out the cold Pad Thai leftovers from yesterday.

There isn't a whole lot left, but I don't feel all that hungry anyway. I don't even bother heating the noodles up.

Instead, I just jam my fork into the slimy things and chew them in silence. What a day.

Minus one friend. My only friend.

It hurts, but honestly not as much as I would've thought. Derek's demeanor helped a lot with that.

Once I'm done shoveling cold leftovers into my mouth, I slip back beneath my covers. It's still early, but I don't care at this point. I just want today to be over.

I spend probably thirty minutes in the dark, trying to drift off with my headphones on when muffled voices from the hallway undo all my efforts.

I'm up in a moment and racing to the door.

Who knows who I'll see out there—with the television blasting, I can't tell who's talking.

Part of me hopes wildly that it's Claire, that she took my warning to heart, and is out there giving it to Victor before telling him it's all over.

I race over to the peephole and manage to get a glimpse of the girl as she slips behind Victor's open door.

Brown hair—it isn't Claire.

It isn't the other brunette from before, either.

How many girls has this been now?

I'm starting to lose track as I hold my breath. Victor is standing in his doorway, one hand on the door while not completely shutting it.

He takes another look over his shoulder, his gaze traveling around the small landing before settling on my door.

He can't possibly know I'm watching, can he?

It feels like I've got a spotlight trained on me, remaining perfectly still, not daring to breathe as I stand in silence. A second later he shuts his door, cutting off my view of whatever's happening inside the apartment.

Claire was just here a few hours ago. Now he's already got a new girl over?

Either he's the most prolific cheater ever, or there's something else going on.

I chew on my lip as I remain by the peephole for another few moments.

There's a battle happening in my exhausted, sleep-deprived brain. Part of me wants to believe that all of this is just in my head, and I'm concocting narratives to fill the emptiness in my own life.

The other part wonders if I'll ever see this girl with the brown hair again.

Finally I pull away from the peephole, my stomach twisted into knots. I take a few steps into the main room and move over to the kitchen sink.

The window just beside me lets in the dull moonlight, illuminating the scratched steel basin at my fingertips.

The TV booms next door, jerking me from my thoughts as the cacophony of noise rips through my brain. Seems like everyone else around here has resigned themselves to their rooms, blissfully ignorant of the rest of the world.

Part of me wonders now if that's on purpose. Maybe people look the other way for their own good.

I don't want to go to sleep, not until I'm sure that girl with the brown hair has left Victor's apartment of her own volition.

It's going to be a battle to stay awake, though. I can already feel my eyelids getting heavier, so drained am I from my interactions today.

I settle down in front of my bed on the floor, knowing if I sit in the bed I'll have no chance.

Turning on the TV, I pull up a horror movie I've seen a few times before. There's enough jump-scares interspersed throughout it should keep my eyes open.

I can't even hear the movie over the level of noise from next door, so I pull on my headphones but don't turn them on. It's just enough to muffle everything so I can focus on reading the subtitles while not completely limiting my hearing.

If voices fill the hallway again, I'll hear them.

The minutes tick by as the movie progresses, a couple of the jump-scares doing enough to spike my heart rate as planned.

My eyelids get heavier as the night drags on. The first movie ends, but there hasn't been any noise from the hallway. It's almost eleven now. I turn on another movie and sit up a little straighter so my back is flush with my bed frame.

The second movie I've seen more than a few times. That was my mistake.

Before I know it, I'm pulling my eyelids back open in a hurry, ripping off my headphones as I whip my head around.

I drifted off, exhaustion having won.

What time is it?

I scramble for my phone, tapping the screen so it will show the time.

11:24.

Straining my hearing, I listen for any sound of commotion from the hallway. It's tough to make out much besides the noise from next door, though. I stand and walk to the peep-hole to peer out at the doors.

Nothing has changed. I let out a breath, telling myself I haven't missed anything. They're still in there, it's not that late.

I walk back and sit down on the floor again, kneading my knuckles into my upper thighs. It's a little painful, but it does the trick to wake me up.

This time, I opt to go without the headphones. It seems even dulling the noise level just a little bit was a big enough chink in my armor for sleep to come.

I pull my head back up to the movie, hardly even able to focus on what's happening on screen with the shared wall rattling and vibrating behind it.

———

It's dark in my apartment, save for the glow coming off the television.

I jerk upright, sucking in a breath.

I fell asleep again. How could I–

There's a noise, and it's not coming from the TV.

Someone is moving in the hallway. I shoot upright, my body aching from having passed out in such a strange position.

I push through the knots in my muscles and stumble to the peephole, completely oblivious to the time.

All I care about is seeing that girl walk out of there. Then I can rest.

I settle in front of the peephole, shutting one eye and pressing the other against the small circle of glass.

What I see *isn't* the brown-haired girl at all.

What I see is much, much worse.

CHAPTER 18

I stare in horror at the sight before me, blinking hard.

It takes a moment for my brain to even comprehend what I'm looking at, but finally I do.

Victor is slightly hunched over, forehead dripping with sweat as he heaves a large black trash bag toward his apartment.

He's got a boot propped in the doorway to hold the door open.

The black plastic bag doesn't move easily. It's taut and looks stuffed nearly to capacity.

I can hardly see straight, but then my wide eye settles on something even more horrifying.

There's a thin trail of blood leaking from the bag.

It's a tiny vein of red that flows across my entire field of vision before disappearing at the staircase.

The smear is dark red. Blood is the only possibility.

With a final grunt, Victor drags the garbage bag across the threshold of his apartment. He straightens back up, his face a little flushed from the effort.

The door closes against the bag, the wood pressing a few

inches into whatever's inside before coming to a stop halfway shut.

Victor is doing something inside. I take a stagger-step backward, my mind reeling.

There's a body in that bag. I'm sure of it.

Blood is leaking. Leaking on the floors. Victor has killed someone, maybe the girl I never saw leave.

I'm not overreacting. *Not at all.*

Victor's footsteps draw me back to the peephole in horrified fascination. I'm terrified, but I can't look away.

He's got a bundle of paper towels in hand. It only takes him a few seconds to wipe up the blood and then he's gone again, slipping inside his apartment and shutting the door with a quiet click.

I can't breathe.

The blood-smeared tile stains my brain.

This time, I don't hesitate to call the cops. It doesn't matter if they bust me for breaking into Victor's mailbox.

Someone is hurt, maybe even killed. If the police come right now, they'll catch Victor before he has a chance to do whatever he plans to do with the trash bag.

I stumble down my hallway, my whole body feeling numb from what I've seen.

I'm delirious with fear. My stomach is so tight I might have thrown up if I'd eaten anything more than a single cup of ramen today.

Where's my phone?

I glance around the dark space wildly, my eyes straining in the dim glow of the TV. Laughter echoes out from next door. Sounds like a prank show or something.

There it is—beneath the pillow on the floor.

I drop down to my knees and scoop the phone up with trembling hands.

It's almost four in the morning. I'd been out for hours. Hours during which Victor did something to that girl.

The realization nearly throws me into the abyss altogether, but I manage to reel my thoughts in enough to unlock my phone and dial the police.

My voice shakes as I wait for an operator to pick up. Finally one does.

"Nine-one-one, what's your emergency?"

I swallow hard, feeling as if there are blades in my throat. "I… my neighbor—I just saw him dragging a big trash bag into his apartment. There was blood leaking out of it. I—I think he's hurt someone."

"Ma'am, what's your address?" the woman asks immediately.

I tell her, shutting my eyes as I speak aloud the address I was so grateful for just a few short days ago.

Now I'm in a nightmare I can't seem to wake up from.

I feel hollow as the call ends. I'm staring blankly at the TV, not paying attention in the slightest.

To their credit, it doesn't take the police long to arrive at all.

I can see the red and blue lights splashing across the brick outside my windows when they park. I stand in a hurry, pressing up against the glass to try and get a look down the alley at the cops.

One of the cruisers is parked right in front of the alley, its lights flashing overhead.

My heart leaps up into my throat. This is it. They're actually here.

I feel almost wooden as I stagger back to the peephole. I can hear steps on the stairwell, hurried and frantic.

There's shouting.

I can hear it even over the blaring of the TV next door—which suddenly cuts its volume drastically, making the commotion outside my apartment sound all the more jarring.

Of course they're willing to turn the television down once the police arrive.

I hardly even think about next door anymore in my haste to get to the peephole as a thunderous pounding starts up.

"Police, open up," a loud voice calls out.

It's happening.

I don't know what to feel. Terror, tension, relief—all of it is sloshing inside of me, my whole body feeling as though I'm on the verge of snapping.

Peering out is a challenge, I'm breathing so heavily. It takes me a moment to focus, but finally I'm able to zero in on the police as they continue to shout for Victor to open the door.

There are four officers, all of them with their guns drawn. One of them is slamming the back of his fist into the wood.

To my surprise, the door comes open a few inches.

The police burst inside like a tidal wave, shoving the door all the way open.

"Get on the ground," one of them shouts.

The words echo through the hallway.

I can't see what's going on behind the cop's bodies. One of the police officers remains outside, drawing his hand across his forehead as he darts his eyes around the hall.

Victor's door bounces off the inside wall and begins to swing closed again, making it about halfway before stopping.

"Don't move," one of the cops shouts.

"What's going on?"

That's Victor, his voice muffled.

I imagine the officers with their bodies holding him down, pressing his face into the old wood flooring.

"Be quiet," one of the cops shouts.

"Peterson, check the kitchen," another says.

Heavy footsteps. More muffled sounds of a struggle.

"Davidson."

The cop standing outside snaps his head up. "Yeah?"

"Come in here."

Davidson eases the door open and steps inside, allowing

me a momentary glimpse into the hallway of Victor's apartment.

Two of the cops have him pinned against the floor, arms twisted around behind him.

Then Davidson shuts the door behind him, and I'm completely cut off.

The hallway falls eerily quiet once again, especially considering the lack of noise from next door.

I press my ear against the wood, shutting my eyes to try and pick up anything I can.

It's no good. Whatever is going on in there, I can't tell from out here.

I need to know.

As gently as I can, I crack open my door and slip out into the hallway. With the quiet, my Crocs squeak across the tile and create enough noise to send my pulse skyrocketing.

I come up against the other wall, heart pounding in my chest.

Did they hear me?

I remain poised, ready in an instant to leap back across the distance to my door, which remains open a crack.

No one comes out.

After another couple seconds, I slowly lower my ear to the wood.

If I'm caught, I'm not sure what I'll say.

Even that is not enough to deter me. I need to know what's going on.

CHAPTER 19

"——t?" a muffled voice asks.

It's one of the police officers.

To my surprise, he doesn't sound alarmed or agitated like I would've expected.

I readjust my position so that my ear is completely flush against the wood.

"—about that," I hear Victor say.

His tone is light, joking. Not what I'd expect to be hearing from a man who's been caught with a body in a trash bag.

He must be putting on a real good show for the cops in there. Playing innocent, friendly.

Or have I got this whole thing completely wrong?

"Sorry about the trouble, we'll speak to her," one of the policemen says.

I blink. They're talking about *me*. My throat is so dry, I nearly cough as I try to swallow.

"It's really not a big deal," Victor says, surprising me.

There's no way he's coming to my aid. He's still trying to garner some goodwill with the police, no doubt.

Mind your own business, you'll regret what happens if you don't.

He's got them all completely fooled.

There's a few more words exchanged that I can't catch. Footsteps.

I realize almost too late they're coming right at me—in another few seconds, they'll be outside.

Pushing off the door, I race back across the hall, just managing to shut my door with a click as Victor's is pulled open. I stare through the peephole, seeing three of the officers filing out.

The fourth says one final thing to Victor, and then steps out to join the rest of the officers.

I swallow again, unable to tear my eyes away.

The men talk among themselves in low voices, one of them flipping through a small notebook before nudging his chin at the stairs.

Three of the cops start toward the stairs, a radio warbling to life. The tinny voice echoes in time with their footsteps as they begin the climb down.

The fourth flips back a page in his notebook, his head coming up to glance at the two doors on my side of the hall.

He's looking for *me*.

There's a small squeak as his boots move across the tile.

He seems to move almost in slow motion as he comes toward my door, his figure growing larger and larger in the view of the peephole until he completely obscures it.

A sharp knock on the wood.

I jerk back, breathing heavily.

He knows I'm definitely awake, seeing as I called the police less than twenty minutes ago and no one goes to sleep after calling the cops.

I chew my lip as the seconds tick by.

Part of me doesn't want to open the door at all. The last thing I need is the judgmental eyes of some cop boring down into me.

Still, I need to know what happened. I need to know how Victor got away with murder.

With a quivering hand, I pull open the door a few inches.

"Ms. Ripley?" he asks.

He's taller than me by a good few inches, the man's form filling the gap between the door.

I look up at him and give a small nod.

He nods in return and then tilts the cap on his head slightly.

"As you no doubt heard, we went next door to Mr. Popov's. There was no body in a trash bag," he says.

"But the blood," I reply.

My mind is racing. *No body?*

The officer shakes his head. "We did locate a black trash bag, though it was filled with just that—trash. Looking through it, it seems some old meat was leaking the blood you saw."

A trash bag filled only with trash. I lean against the door, feeling a little lightheaded.

Is it possible I'm really this wrong? Have I conjured a killer out of my own mind?

"So you… didn't find anything," I say quietly.

The cop glances down at his sheet of paper. "Besides a few non-prescription pills that aren't worth the time it would take to file the paperwork, no."

I refuse to believe it. The bloody shirts, the multiple women…

"If it was just trash, why was he dragging it *into* his apartment, as opposed to taking it out?" I ask.

The officer nodded. "Mr. Popov explained that too. He'd brought out the trash, only to realize he'd accidentally tossed a receipt he needed with it. He was bringing it back inside to dig through and locate the receipt."

I let out a breath. It's a perfectly plausible explanation, and I can't argue it. Maybe I really am losing my mind.

"Okay," I say finally.

There isn't much else I can do. If Victor did do something wrong, he's clearly smarter than the police. Even more troubling is the idea that he didn't do anything wrong at all, and I've called the cops over nothing.

Glancing up at the officer, I find that he's regarding me with a similar look of pity to Derek's. He gives a short nod and then claps his notebook shut.

"Have a good night, Ma'am," the officer says, stepping back.

I close my door and lock the deadbolt, turning until my back is flush with the wall.

I slide down it until my butt hits the wood floor. Nothing but trash in the bag. Meat was the source of the blood.

My palms come up to press into my eye sockets as I rub them, creating little dots that dance across my vision. Maybe I do just need to sleep.

My door shudders as a sudden pounding starts up against it, sending me sprawling.

"Salem," Victor hisses from the other side.

"I know it was you. I know it was you who called the cops."

CHAPTER 20

can't move.

Victor standing in front of my door blocks any light from seeping through underneath.

I can see him standing there in my mind, his hulking frame pulsing with rage.

"Open up the door," he hisses.

I scramble backwards, my sweatpants catching on the rough wood. The fabric tears as I jerk, the rip like rolling thunder in the silence.

It only serves to agitate Victor more as he pounds against the wooden surface.

For once, I'm thankful for the heavy, old door. It holds up against the beating, allowing me to stumble backwards into my dark apartment.

"Salem, open the door," Victor's voice calls after me.

I know if I do, it'd be a huge mistake.

He's still there, pounding away, even as I wrap my fingers around my headphones and pull them back on.

Tears are streaming down my face as I turn them on, trying to block out the noise.

I'm so terrified I feel physically ill.

Not only have I failed to stop Victor, now he's trained his focus on me.

I don't know how he managed to hide the body from the police. Maybe he was prepared for something like this and had a bag of trash ready to go.

Somehow, he's gotten away with murder.

He's smart, dangerous. Now, he's after me.

I'm lying on my bed now, the comforter pulled up to my chin as my headphones blare music. I don't know if Victor is still at the door.

It doesn't matter much.

I don't ever plan to step foot outside this apartment again.

CHAPTER 21

Victor

Now she's done it.

My last pound against her door goes unanswered like all the rest. It's past five AM now, and I'm exhausted.

Salem isn't going to answer the door. She's in there, though.

Hiding. Watching.

She should've listened to me. She should've stayed away, minded her own business. Whatever happens to her now isn't my fault.

I turn away from her door with a huff, stalking back over to my side of the hall. Adrenaline still courses through my body from the police's visit.

They were so close to discovering the truth.

My hand flexes as I pull open my door and step inside.

Even now when I shut my eyes, I can hear their shouts at the door. The utter panic that ran through me at their appearance.

I didn't have long at all to cover up what I'd done. If they'd found out the truth, everything would have collapsed.

My door clicks shut behind me, leaving me standing in the

dark. I take a slow breath, working hard to reign myself back in.

They're gone now. The only issue remaining is with Salem.

Calling the police was a big mistake. She'll pay for it soon enough.

I take a few steps down my hallway until I'm in the main room of my apartment. All of the lights are off.

It allows me to see the small red dot of the camera in the corner clearly. Luckily, the police didn't notice.

I didn't need them asking me any more questions.

One look at the filthy trash, and they were satisfied. I even asked if they wanted to search through it themselves, but they declined.

I round the corner and settle against my kitchen counter, crossing my arms in front of me.

They didn't find out the truth.

My gaze falls on the far side of the room, where a small couch is pressed against the wall. Funny that brunette— Vanessa?—noticed how small the room seemed.

She was more right than she knew.

Luckily for me, the police didn't comment on it at all.

I push off the counter and cross to the other side, coming to a stop in front of the couch.

My breathing slows even further as I stare at the wall.

The couch lets out a small squeak as I push it to the side to expose the secret door.

I know exactly what is waiting for me in the small room hidden behind the faux wall. It turns my stomach to think about what I need to do, but I don't have any choice.

I've got to do what needs to be done.

CHAPTER 22

I turn over in the bed, cracking a bleary eyelid as the light streams in through my curtainless windows.

My head is pounding from the lack of sleep. It's just after seven AM. I was out only a couple hours at the most.

Already though, I know I won't be able to go back to sleep. It'll be impossible.

I pull the sheets back up over me protectively as the events of last night come roaring back in my mind.

When I pull my headphones off, I'm almost expecting to hear Victor still pounding at the door.

It's quiet, though. I swallow and push myself up, wincing a little at a sharp pain in my hand.

Another splinter in my palm, the small sliver of wood surrounded by angry red skin.

I didn't even notice it last night, having been much more concerned with Victor sounding like he intended to break my door down and punish me for nearly getting him caught.

Now though, I can feel the splinter clearly. There are a few drops of dried blood on my sheets and pillowcase, making me groan inwardly at the thought of having to go do laundry.

That means leaving the apartment. It means going out there... facing him.

The only way I'll leave is if I'm sure Victor is out. Even then, I don't ever intend to step out for more than a few minutes.

The buzzing of my phone jars me. I pat a hand around the bed to locate the source of the hum, my fingers closing around the phone a second later.

Through my bleary eyes, I see who's calling.

It's Derek.

My stomach sinks as his weird demeanor last night settles on me again. No doubt he's calling to apologize, but I won't hear it.

I let the call go to voicemail as I turn and get my feet onto the floor. My Crocs have been tossed haphazardly a few feet away, so I lean over to pull them toward me with a yawn.

Stuffing my feet inside, I can't help but glance at my phone screen as it buzzes again.

A text from Derek.

I was way out of line last night, Salem.

I don't respond. Words aren't going to take away the sinking feeling I get in my chest every time I think about his hungry gaze on me.

With a sigh, I flip the phone over. My stomach rumbles loudly. I didn't eat last night with everything that went on.

This morning, I'm feeling the effects. My stomach aches, crying out for food now that I'm waking up.

I move over to the cabinet and pry it open. My heart does a flip in my chest. I've got no more food, besides a couple dry crackers.

My stomach tightens as my vision swims a little bit. I definitely need to think about getting something in my stomach.

I'm still staring at the empty cupboard as a heavy door creaking open snaps me to attention.

Is that Victor?

I'm up to the peephole in a few steps and am just able to catch the top of his head as he heads down the stairs.

I remain at the door another few seconds, listening to the sound of his boots on the steps fading away.

Part of me wonders if it's some sort of trick to draw me out. That he's waiting on the second-floor landing for me, eyes wild and shirt soaked in blood.

I swallow hard as my stomach tightens again. I need to order food.

My hands shake as I open up the delivery app, I'm that hungry. Within a few seconds I've got the bare essentials ordered and my credit card entered to pay for them.

I don't even want to know what I owe on the card. Checking and seeing how much I owe might actually make me vomit right now.

Twenty minutes until the order can be delivered. I pace back and forth, willing the hall to stay quiet.

Victor hasn't come back, which means he really did go out. I can only hope he's out for long enough.

My phone dings again, and I pick it up, expecting to see a message from the delivery driver.

Instead it's Derek again.

Salem, please respond. I'm sorry about everything I said.

I swipe out of the text message and go back to the delivery app, refreshing every few seconds as I tap my foot.

I'm guzzling water to try and fill the cavern that has opened up in my stomach. It helps a little, but I need real food.

Finally my phone buzzes again—the delivery guy is on his way.

Every second feels tense as I wait in the kitchen, taking small sips of water each time my stomach grumbles.

I try to push Derek's texts out of mind. With everything else going on right now, dealing with him is the last thing I want to be doing.

Hurriedly I pull on my trench coat in anticipation of the cold breeze that'll hit me when I open the door for the delivery.

My hand clutches my phone like a lifeline as I watch the small shopping cart icon traveling across Williamsburg toward me. It shows where the delivery driver is.

He's almost here.

I want to time it just right so that I won't have to spend a minute more outside my apartment than I absolutely have to.

The little cart draws closer, seeming to move at a snail's pace as I pace back and forth in the kitchen.

He's on my street. I tighten my coat and grab a beanie off the countertop.

Suddenly the cart zips forward—and past my apartment. It continues up the street, even as I shout at my phone to stop.

The guy missed my building.

I watch the cart icon pause at an intersection for a moment, and then it spins and begins heading to the left.

"No, wrong way," I hiss at the screen.

My knuckles are white as I clutch my phone.

The cart is coming back down toward me, only one street over. My phone thrums in my hand as a call comes through the app.

The delivery guy is lost.

"You're on the wrong street," I say as I pick up.

"Okay, sorry," the man says in broken English.

I rub my forehead, realizing my words came out a little harsh. "I'm sorry. I'm just tired. I'll be down in a minute."

I pace to the front door again, peering through the peep hole a moment. Once I'm satisfied the coast is clear, I pull open the door and slip out.

It shuts behind me as I race down the stairs, my heart pounding.

Victor isn't anywhere to be seen.

The second stairwell is empty, as is the first floor. It's as quiet as a graveyard, in complete opposition to last night when the police busted inside.

I shoot down the main hallway, pushing thoughts of my last conversation with Claire out of mind.

Her words still hurt a little.

You're crazy.

I hold my phone up again to see the little cart rounding the corner. I'm waiting in the small vestibule between the buildings two entry doors, face up against the glass of the front door as I peer outside.

I still don't see the delivery guy.

I check the app again and see that the cart is now two streets back. A hiss escapes my mouth as I dial up the delivery guy this time.

"I'm sorry," he says immediately as the line connects.

"It's okay," I say, trying to keep myself calm.

Victor's not here, I'm okay.

I pull on the handle for the front door, which thankfully opens without issue.

A blast of cold October air slices right through my trench coat like it's not even there.

I'm forced to take a step back as I blink hard, my eyes filled with tears at the sudden temperature change from the warmth of the building.

Breathing heavily, I flip up my collar and step onto the front steps with the phone to my ear.

"Do you see me?" I ask.

I can hear horns in the background of the call and in real life.

"Sorry, no," the man says a second later.

"I'm waving my arm," I add.

"Okay… yes, I see," the man says finally.

Relief floods through me. There he is, coming down the street on a motorized bike with a dented red helmet. He pulls off the street and up onto the sidewalk as I trot down the steps and draw open the gate.

"For Sal... *Sall-um*?" he asks in a hesitant voice.

"Yes."

He nods and moves around to the back of his bike, where a small thermobox holds my groceries.

Unzipping the top, he heaves out the first bag with a grunt. It's packed to the brim, a stick of butter coming off the top of the pile and landing on the concrete beside us.

I take the bag, caught off-guard by how heavy it is as my muscles kick in to compensate. I ordered enough for a few weeks so that I wouldn't have to go outside again, but didn't think about the logistics of getting that many groceries inside.

He pulls out a second, equally bulging bag and hands it over. Between the two of them, my arms are already starting to burn from the workout.

"Thanks," I say through gritted teeth.

The man gives me a nod and then is already zooming back onto the street.

He narrowly avoids a collision with a car as it screeches to a halt, laying on the horn when the man shoots down the road.

I turn back to my apartment with a bag in each hand. Suddenly a pop fills the air, and my load is instantly lighter.

I look up at the sky overhead, fighting back the urge to scream that threatens to take over.

The last thing I need is my groceries spilled out across the sidewalk. I'm sleep-deprived, terrified, and freezing with this wind that just keeps on blowing.

A can of soup is already trying to make its escape as it begins to roll to my right, the metal clattering over the uneven sidewalk.

I set down the bags in a hurry and take off after it, cheeks burning at the thought of anyone watching this embarrassing show.

It comes to a stop in front of a small cafe. Two women with ponytails are peering over the tops of their laptops at me, their mouths curled into smiles.

Clearly they're laughing at me. I grab the can of soup and stuff it into my pocket before turning on a heel and heading back toward the grocery pile on the sidewalk.

The first bag has a pretty good rip in the bottom of it, but after dumping everything out, I manage to tie it off enough that it holds. It's not pretty, but I don't care. I just want to get back inside.

Hastily I throw everything back into the bag and climb back to my feet, balancing the two heavy parcels in my arms.

I amble toward the gate and prop it open with a foot, sliding myself inside before stepping up to the front door.

As I dig around my pockets for the key however, my stomach drops.

As scatter-brained as I am today, I've forgotten my keys.

CHAPTER 23

can't help it, I start crying.

I just feel beaten.

The tears threaten to overwhelm me as I stand there, hungry and tired and shivering in the cold.

My Crocs do nothing to stave off the wind that pushes hard against my back, blowing my collar up into my cheeks.

Maybe someone will come out and let me in. I peer through the glass but don't see anyone in the hallway.

Come to think of it, besides Victor and his cadre of girls, I've never really seen much of anyone at all. It's a whole building of shut-ins like me.

I rack my brain for what to do.

Then it hits me, but so does a wave of nausea at the thought. My spare key is with Derek.

I let out a sigh as I step away from the door and exit the gate again.

A tall tree overhead rustles in the breeze, a few dead leaves fluttering down and landing on the graffitied cement at my feet.

As much as I don't want to have anything to do with him ever again, I've got to get that key back. I've also got to do it before Victor returns to the building, which means the clock is ticking.

I don't want to be caught out here alone with him, despite the daylight. It's early, and I don't see anyone else out in the street with me.

It takes effort to shuffle over to the trash cans lined against the side of the building and set my bundles of groceries down on top.

Once my arms are free, I let out a relieved breath and grab my phone. The wind hits me again, making my fingers go numb as I swipe up on the screen.

I stare at Derek's name, and the unanswered texts I've gotten from him. It's the absolute last thing I want to do, but I have no other choice.

———

The cafe is mostly quiet as I wait for Derek to arrive.

It's just me and two couples, both of whom are snuggled up together and engaged in low conversation in different corners of the restaurant.

Given how Derek acted the last time I saw him, I didn't feel comfortable having him meet me in front of my place. A super public setting like this cafe will be much better.

Not like I expect him to try something, but I'm on edge. A place like this has cameras, and that makes me feel a whole lot better.

Wisps of steam rise off the top of the coffee that sits in front of me. I haven't had a single sip of it.

My mind is way too preoccupied with getting back inside my apartment before Victor returns. This cafe is two streets over, but with a view of the walk back from the nearest subway station.

When I'd asked for the key, Derek texted back and said he was working in the area today and could meet me soon.

That was almost twenty minutes ago.

The minutes continue to tick by, each one furthering the anxiety that builds within my chest. I want to be back inside my apartment, behind a locked door.

Though it's a bright fall day, I don't feel it. My mind reels, my stomach rumbles.

My bags of groceries are stacked together at the base of my chair. If this goes on for much longer, there's a good chance I'll lose some of the items I've bought that need to be refrigerated.

The door dings open behind me.

It's Derek, wearing his sanitation department uniform and a high-vis vest on top of it. The highlighter yellow vest clashes with the dark walls of the cafe.

He rubs his hands together as he looks around the room before spotting me and heading over. I can feel myself stiffening as he approaches.

My palms feel sweaty all of a sudden. He was the one who messed up, so why do I feel so embarrassed?

"Hi," Derek starts.

I can hardly look up at him, glancing at his face for only a second before shifting my eyes back to the table.

"Hi. Did you bring the key?"

He nods and pulls out the massive key ring that always hangs at his hip. It drops to the table with a metallic clank.

"Listen, Sal. About the other day…" he begins.

It's not loud enough in here to have any sort of private conversation. Besides, I don't want to deal with this right now. I need to get back to my apartment.

"It's fine," I say quickly, just wanting to get this over with.

I can feel his eyes on me again, willing me to look up at him. Finally I do, my eyes finding his.

"I was way too drunk, and said some stuff I shouldn't have."

I squirm in my chair. "Can I have the keys, please?"

Derek reaches toward the key ring and begins to sift through them. My eyes continually flick out to the street outside, wondering if at any moment I'll see Victor heading back toward the apartment.

"I just… I thought you liked me back," Derek continues.

He's paused the key search.

Clearly, he really wants to talk about this. I chew my lip, willing his fingers to start going through the keys again.

Why has he stopped? Does he think stalling is going to improve my perception of him?

I look up at him again and wrap my fingers around my coffee cup for protection. The warmth of it fills me with a sense of strength.

"I'm sorry, but I've *never* seen you that way, Derek."

I hope my words will be enough to placate him, and he'll keep sorting through the keys. To my dismay, he sets down the key ring altogether and leans closer to me.

"Why not, Salem? Am I that ugly?"

His words come out rushed, making my heart beat faster. I glance around the cafe, but no one nearby seems to have heard our conversation.

"I… I just don't like you like that," I say, my voice coming out in little more than a squeak.

"That's not good enough," Derek says loudly through gritted teeth.

The words come out loud enough to pull up the barista's head toward us. I make eye contact with the girl, whose eyebrows flick up questioningly.

"Sorry, sorry," Derek says, breathing out a little.

I look him over again. He seems on edge, like he's close to doing something. His leg bounces up and down beneath the table, his boot making a squeaking sound on the floor with each motion.

The barista is still looking in my direction. I glance over at her, making eye contact again.

"Please just give me the key, Derek," I say, my voice trembling.

Derek runs a hand through his hair and takes a breath as he licks his lips. "I'm not—you've got me all wrong, Sal. I'm just saying, I've been nothing but a good guy to you. For years."

"Is everything okay over here?"

Both our heads turn to the barista, who stands beside our table. Her presence drains the tension away like air from a balloon.

The girl looks down at me, seeking my eyes.

"He's giving me my key back," I say.

Both of us look to Derek, who opens his mouth again and then closes it. With a third party involved now, he has no choice but to hand over the key. It's a good thing too, because my heart is pounding so hard I think I'd spill the coffee if I tried to take a sip.

Derek's jaw muscles pulse as he sifts through the ring of keys, his eyes flashing up to me every couple of seconds. I don't want to look at him anymore. I want to be back home. This has gone on way too long already.

Finally, he stops on one key and pulls it off before placing it on the table. His fingers cover it. He looks like he wants to say one last thing.

"Sal…"

"I'm sorry, Derek," I reply.

I'm not sorry, but I know it's something I have to say for this to be over. Derek looks up at the barista again, who has a smile frozen across her face.

She looks completely unfazed, standing still as a statue as Derek pushes the key toward me.

I'm so thankful for her, I could cry.

After another second, Derek presses his palms to the tabletop and stands.

"Fine," he says, sounding disgruntled. "Fine. But don't

expect me to come running next time you need my help with anything."

Then he's gone, stalking away toward the front door. It opens with a ding and lets in a shock of cold air before coming shut behind him.

"Thank you," I say to the barista, whose name tag reads *Amy*.

Amy gives me a small smile. "No problem. I knew something was up the moment he came in here. Us girls gotta have each other's back."

I manage a smile of my own before scooping up my key and stuffing it into my pocket. Amy heads back behind the counter, leaving me to gather up my groceries and race back to my apartment.

I spent way too long here with Derek, not to mention the time it actually took for him to arrive. Finally though, I have a key. I'm home free.

Using my butt, I push open the café door and start down the sidewalk again. The wind tears into me, blasting my face and making my cheeks start to go numb as I fight my way up the sidewalk. I just want to be back in my room.

At any moment, I expect Victor to pop out from behind a car with a snarl across his face.

The streets remain empty, though. I make it back to my apartment building and glance up at it. It reveals nothing.

In a moment I'm back inside and shooting down the hall. The home stretch. I scamper up the stairs, taking them as quickly as my legs can manage before finally arriving on the third floor again.

It's empty, allowing me to let out a breath I'd been involuntarily holding. As I step closer to my apartment however, I blink. The door is slightly ajar.

My pulse quickens. *Thump-thump. Thump-thump.*

Did I leave it like that? I know I didn't lock it, because I didn't have my keys. I also didn't expect to be out for as long as I was.

I draw closer, my legs having turned to stone.

Each of my footsteps seems to echo in my mind as I walk.

I brace my shoulder against the door, hardly able to hear anything around my pulse in my ears.

Is Victor waiting for me inside?

I nudge the door open with a toe, the old wood letting out a creak as it swings.

What I see sucks the air right out of my lungs.

CHAPTER 24

The apartment is utterly trashed.

All of my meager belongings are strewn across the floor. The TV screen is cracked and shattered, bits of glass scattered on the wood boards. I look to my bed, where the sheets have been ripped off.

Even the drawers in the kitchen have been opened, my utensils tossed around the room.

Then I see the microwave. Its door is hanging off the hinge, and the interior plate is cracked in two.

My whole apartment has been utterly wrecked. I sag against the counter, swallowing hard as I shut my eyes.

My immediate thought is that Victor has done this to get back at me. I call the cops, he trashes my apartment.

Then another thought wracks my body. It did take Derek forever to meet me at the coffee shop, even though he said he was in the area. He still had my key with him at that point, and that means he could've unlocked the front door and let himself inside.

I shake my head. No, he wouldn't have done this. What would be the point of wrecking my room only to beg for my forgiveness again?

I rub my face with my hands.

Instead of breaking down into tears again however, I feel something else building within me. A burning in my chest I haven't felt since Mom.

A person can only take so much. I'm tired of being kicked around and treated like this. The TV was all I had.

My fists curl up as I set my brow. I'm done.

Somehow this final act has pushed me over the edge of terrified and into some new realm. I've dug deeper than rock bottom. There isn't much worse that could happen to me, and somehow that fills me with a sense of indignation that wasn't there only moments ago.

I step out of the room again, jaw clenched.

I almost hope Victor is watching through his peephole as I stare down the door. I'm done being afraid.

I march down the stairs again, my footsteps landing hard on each step.

My hand comes down against the wood of the super's door. Basically everything in my apartment is broken now. Not to mention I'd like him to pull up the security footage so I can confirm it was Victor who trashed my apartment.

The knock goes unanswered however, once again. I pound on the door with the flat of my palm, the sound echoing through the first floor.

My cheeks burn. It's getting ridiculous at this point. The owner of this building needs to fire the super and hire a new one.

After another minute passing without any response from the guy, I reach over to the wall and rip off one of the sheets hung there. It's some list of emergency numbers to call. I flip the paper over and scribble out a note for the super.

Room 5B. Oven, microwave broken. Have also had apartment vandalized. Please call me here.

I write out my number and then slip the paper under the door.

Back in my apartment, I get to work putting everything back where it belongs. It takes me less than an hour, because I don't have a whole lot of things to begin with. One of my two forks is bent, rendering it useless.

I clutch it between my hands, feeling that burning sensation rise up in my stomach again. This has to stop, one way or another.

I can't keep going like this.

My mind drifts back to Claire, and how poorly our last conversation went. I can't have that happen again—it might cost her her life.

Just because I couldn't convince her the first time around, I won't let that deter me. Not this time.

––––––

I blink hard to wet my dry eyes that have been staring at the computer screen for way too long.

I've spent the past couple hours scouring the news for any mention of murdered women who fit the description of the girls I'd seen.

It has proved to be fruitless. Whatever Victor is doing to them, he's managed to keep it out of the news. I already knew he was smart, and this is just further proof. I've also done some more thinking on how to broach the topic with Claire again.

It's clear she won't listen to me face-to-face, so I've decided to gather up what I can and mail it to her. I'll include Victor's arrest record, as well as anything I can find in the news.

I just need to figure out her address.

It takes time to locate Victor's social media. Finally I locate a single profile under the name Victor Popov who is in New York City.

There's only a single image of him up, and it was posted

four years ago. Clearly, he isn't too big of a fan of social media. That checks out, considering he's probably trying to stay under the radar.

It's definitely Victor in the picture though, his long arm around the shoulder of a slightly shorter girl also with dark hair. Probably an old girlfriend.

Under the account's list of friends, I find what I'm looking for.

Claire Williams.

Unlike Victor, Claire's social media are filled with images of her. She's even posted something today, sharing an image of her at some restaurant with a plate of food in front of her.

I can see in the top of the photo there's another plate too. That explains where Victor went this morning.

A sweet little brunch. My stomach twists at the thought of Victor seated across from Claire, his cold eyes watching her while she takes a photo.

Has he threatened her the way he's threatened me?

Other posts are inspirational quotes and scenic shots of Claire smiling brightly all around New York City. She looks so happy.

I can't let something happen to her—I need to warn her before it's too late.

Now that I know her name, I can figure out where she lives. Navigating back over to my law firm's website, I open up the tool that tracks down addresses.

I type in Claire Williams and input New York City as a location before waiting for the screen to load.

Once it does, I find what I'm looking for.

She lives in the East Village, not more than a few subway stops away from here.

I sit back, feeling a sense of relief wash over me now that I've got her address. The only issue now is that I don't really have all that much to send her.

Showing up on her doorstep and demanding she listen to

me is most certainly not the way to approach this. That's a one-way ticket right back to a mental institution.

I haven't found anything on the web about the girls, either. I have no concrete proof of what Victor's up to, only my suspicions.

Unfortunately, those won't be enough to convince anyone. Not Claire, not the police, not even myself.

I have to know the truth, and there's only one way I can think of to find it out.

If there is indeed something going on in Apartment 6B, I *will* figure out what.

Even if it means risking everything.

CHAPTER 25

Maybe I really am losing my mind.

That's the only explanation I can think of as to why I'm seriously considering breaking into Victor's apartment.

Even just the thought makes my throat tighten. Still, I know it's what I have to do.

Everything he does, he does in that apartment. Somehow he was able to keep his actions hidden from the police.

If I'm going to find proof I can use to help persuade Claire, it'll be across the hall.It's really my only choice, although it utterly terrifies me.

What if he catches me? What if I'm entirely wrong altogether?

The thought has crossed my mind more than once. Everyone around me thinks Victor is not a problem. Derek, Claire, even the police.

The fact that there aren't any missing or murdered women matching the girl's descriptions doesn't help either.

So for my own sanity, I've got to break in and find out what's going on once and for all.

If it costs me my freedom, so be it. Because if I'm right, I might just be able to stop a killer before he hurts anyone else.

Once the decision is made, I have nothing to do but wait. The hours pass agonizingly slowly. I also don't know if Victor is in or out, since I only heard his door close this morning when he went out for brunch with Claire.

That thought brings my head up.

Maybe there's a way I can know if he's in or out.

I pull up Claire's social media again, moving through all her accounts for any updates on what she's been up to today.

She posts with almost startling frequency, allowing me to be clued in to her whereabouts.

Claire last posted something two hours ago, a picture of the red and yellow trees in Central Park, complete with plenty of emojis.

Unfortunately, it's impossible to know if Victor is there with her, because I don't see him in the photo.

I lower the phone with a sigh and rub my temples.

If Victor did trash my room, I just have to assume he's in his apartment now.

Based on his usual patterns, he seems to leave later in the night and return shortly thereafter with a new girl in tow.

Maybe that'll be the case tonight, too.

Waiting for darkness to fall seems to take forever, but I know it's coming soon when the TV next door starts up right on cue. The noise rips through the thin wall, snapping my head toward it even though I've come to expect it.

With the show playing, I won't be able to hear if Victor leaves. The slamming of my palm against the shared wall does nothing, as usual. It's routine at this point—the television plays, I pound the wall, nothing changes.

Still, I won't be deterred. Grabbing a protein bar and a bag of pumpkin candy corn, I march over to my door.

I'm on a stakeout, and I'll need snacks.

I won't leave this spot until I know for sure that Victor has left his apartment.

Another hour passes without any signs of movement whatsoever in the hallway.

It really is kind of weird how quiet it gets out there, when I drown out the noise from next door.

Truly a building of introverts.

Finally around seven PM, I hear something. Only it's not coming from Victor's room. It's coming from the staircase.

A man in his thirties is making his way down the stairs, his skin heavily marked with tattoos. He's even got a couple on the sides of his face.

He has shoulder length hair with only the last two inches or so dyed blonde. Clearly, it's been a while since he went in and reupped.

He shuffles down the steps with his hands in his pockets, a slack look across his face.

I get the feeling that if I were to try and greet him, I'd receive the same blank stare I've gotten from others in the building.

The man hits the third-floor landing and continues down the steps, his shoulders slumped. Another few seconds, and he's disappeared entirely from view.

I'm left staring at the two doors across the hall again. After another hour of nothing happening, I might as well be staring at a painting.

I stretch my body, wincing a little at the tightness in my back. The peephole is at the perfect height to be aggravating.

Clearly, the designers of these things did not intend to have the user staring through it for hours on end.

Still, here I am. When ten o'clock hits, I start to wonder if Victor isn't going to come out at all.

Then, almost as if summoned by magic, I see his door swinging inward as he pulls it open.

I suck in a sharp breath, my mind instantly beginning to

race. He's got on washed jeans and a black t-shirt that tells me he doesn't intend on staying out for too long.

In this weather, I wouldn't last more than a few minutes—especially now that it's dark outside, making it even colder.

Victor doesn't seem deterred however, and pulls his door shut behind him. He coughs into his arm and then glances toward my door.

Every atom in my body freezes at his look.

Does he see me? Does he know I'm there?

Then he looks away and starts toward the staircase, allowing me to let out a small breath. I wait an entire minute before daring to move a muscle.

When I'm finally certain that Victor has gone, only then do I start thinking again.

My thoughts continue to hammer through my skull.

Should I try now?

I have no idea how long he'll be out. Maybe he's just running to pick up food, like I've done. I'd hardly have more than a couple minutes to look around before he returned.

I remain behind the door, the seconds ticking on. I'm torn between scampering across the hallway and getting inside, and the thoughts screaming that I'll be caught the moment I do.

It's impossible to know how much time I'd have.

Even worse is the thought that each moment I spend deliberating is less time. The seconds and minutes pass by as I remain frozen by indecision.

He could be back at any minute now. After four minutes, I curse myself for not just going immediately. The time I've spent standing here could've been spent searching his apartment for clues.

I don't know when I'll have another chance to investigate. With a start, I realize Claire might not have another chance either. If I'm not able to provide proof soon, Victor might do something to her.

This could be my last chance.

After another two minutes, I can't stand it anymore. Clearly he isn't just picking up food from the front door. That means I have at least a couple minutes.

I swallow around the lump in my throat and move my trembling hand to the deadbolt to unlock it.

Then I pull my hoodie over my head, not like it really matters. If Victor figures out someone has been in his apartment and checks the tapes, he'll see immediately that it was me who entered.

Still, having the hood on makes me feel more secure. I've got a pair of gloves on too, just to be as careful as possible.

It's absolutely vital I don't disturb anything more than I have to. Without knowing how long I have, I need to be in and out as quickly as possible.

That means I can't waste another minute deliberating.

I literally don't have the time to spare.

My door is open, and then I'm moving across the tile to the other side of the hall. The noise from the TV is a little less blaring in the hallway, but still enough that it covers the sounds of my door shutting.

I realize with a start it'll obscure the noise of Victor coming back, too.

That freezes me against his door. What other choice do I have, though?

I need to know the truth.

If Victor is hiding something, I need to know. Lives may very well depend on it.

With another breath, I fish out the paperclip from my pocket and drop down to a knee so that I can pick the lock.

The click as it unlocks runs through me. I stand, my fingers coming to rest against the doorknob as I take a final look around.

Then I'm slipping inside, my heart pounding.

CHAPTER 26

My breathing comes in short gasps.

The apartment is dark and quiet before me as I stand in the hallway. Gently I let the door shut and lock it behind me.

Then I turn back around, feeling as though a single wrong step will set alarms to ringing.

I creep forward. As I get deeper inside, I realize his apartment is laid out exactly the same as mine, only flipped because he is on the opposite side.

That helps me navigate as I come to the first door on my left, which is the bathroom. I push against the door, a whine escaping the hinge as I do.

The sound freezes me, my breath catching in my throat. Silence meets my ears as I listen in.

I step inside and pull out my phone to activate the flashlight.

The harsh white light illuminates the bathroom, revealing a rather sterile looking space that I'm a little disturbed to find is cleaner than mine.

A quick glance under the sink reveals little more than a few spare rolls of toilet paper. There isn't anything of interest that I can see here.

The seconds tick by in my mind. At any moment, Victor could return.

I step out of the bathroom and continue down the hall, finding myself standing beside the oven.

Before me is the rest of the apartment. I don't dare turn on a light, just in case Victor or someone else were to look up and see it from outside.

I can't even hear the street from here, though. I guess we're high enough up that the noise is reduced. The quiet is haunting and makes me keenly aware of every noise I make as I pass over the kitchen with my light.

The oven is immaculate, like he hasn't ever used it. A level of cleanliness that does nothing to dispel my idea of him as a serial killer, that's for sure.

It also makes my chest pang with worry. If he's this careful about crumbs or stains, what chance do I have of finding something incriminating?

I pass the light over the rest of the kitchen area, finding nothing out of place. It almost feels like I'm in a model home, it's so neat.

My fingers wrap around the first knob to open the cabinets. I inspect them, finding a few spices and boxes of plastic bags. Nothing incriminating.

I go to the silver trash can next, shining my light down into it. It's about halfway full, and the smell doesn't have me particularly eager to sift through.

I'm running out of time. I swallow hard again, barely able to take in a full breath for fear of Victor's return.

If he comes in now, I'd be completely screwed. Judging by how avoidant the rest of the neighbors are, I doubt anyone would come to my aid.

I spin around, telling myself I have less than a minute left before I need to go.

My phone flashlight passes over the rest of the apartment.

Besides the tidy bed, there's a black leather couch, a cream white rug, a glass coffee table, a bookshelf, and finally a dresser against one wall. Some black minimalist art hangs to round out the decor.

All of it matches, but there's no personality. There's also nothing that sticks out to me.

I step over to the dresser, pulling the drawers open and sifting through the clothes in search of anything.

I move quickly, my heart beating so fast I'm afraid I might drop my phone. There's nothing but clothing inside, however.

I'm nearly out of time.

Looking over the room again, my brow furrows. Is it really possible I could've been this wrong?

I've found absolutely nothing that I can use to prove my suspicions to Claire. I'm out of time.

Just as I start to turn, however, I pause. I move the flashlight back over the expanse of the room.

It's the same general layout as mine, yes. But somehow, it appears smaller. My apartment is pretty miniscule to begin with, but as I pass the light around the room, I'm sure this one is even more so.

How is that possible?

I step closer to the couch to get a better look at the wall. It's almost like there's more insulation or something, bringing the walls closer together and shrinking the available square footage.

Why would that be?

The phone light skims down the length of the wall, and that's when I notice it. My heart leaps up into my throat again as my pulse pounds.

There's a tiny cut in the drywall, only noticeable in the dark with a light against it. It looks about as thin as a hair.

I maneuver myself behind the couch, pushing it out just enough so that I can stand flush against the wall.

My mind is screaming at me to leave–*Victor is coming, Victor is coming.*

I've spent way too long here already. Still, I need to know what this is.

I crouch down beside the small hairline crack, brushing my fingers over it.

I let out a little gasp. It's not just a crack–there is a small division here, barely wider than the width of paper.

My fingers run up the length of it. There's definitely something back here.

I trace the outline of it, realizing it's like a small door, no more than three or four feet high.

But how do I open it? I throw a glance over my shoulder, though the apartment is still quiet. Moonlight streams in from the two narrow windows that face the street.

I study the wall again, feeling along the length of the cutout.

Suddenly there's a soft *click*, and the door swings outward. I can hardly focus, my heart is beating so fast.

I have to get onto my hands and knees to crawl into the small space before I can straighten up again and hold up my phone.

There's the real wall, a rough brick that's probably about two feet from my face. Even just being inside here makes me feel claustrophobic, trapped.

Then I see them.

The pair of cuffs built into the wall, the metal catching the light of my phone that reflects off it.

This is no storage space. This is some sort of torture chamber. A prison cell, impossibly small and cramped.

Thoughts of girls with their hands suspended overhead splinter through my mind, their bodies beaten and sagging. I'm going to be sick.

My hands shake so hard, I'm worried the photos I take will be so blurry they won't be any good for Claire.

This is the proof I need. This will convince her I'm not some crazy stalker.

My breath feels caught in my throat as I snap the photos. Even the air in here is stale and carries an odd scent I don't want to place.

Nightmares have happened here. I think back to the police visit a couple days ago.

Victor had probably stuffed the body in here just minutes before they arrived. He was talking to them, laughing and joking while a dead girl's body was stuffed inside the walls.

The thoughts make my vision swirl. I need to get a hold of myself before I pass out in here, and Victor comes back to find me.

Now that I know for certain I'm not going crazy, I'm all the more terrified to be in this apartment. The man is a killer, a sadist. And I've just broken into his apartment.

Once the photos are taken I crawl out of the space, only allowing myself to breathe once I'm back into the main room.

Any sense of relief I feel is sucked out of me the moment I hear footsteps outside the door.

CHAPTER 27

Victor is back.

Unadulterated, primal fear takes over my mind, freezing me as I hear the muffled noise of keys jingling.

He's going to find me. He's going to kill me.

Every atom of my body trembles as I look around desperately in the dark. I've got mere moments until he comes inside.

A metallic clatter followed by a stifled curse tells me he's dropped the keys. I need to hide. I need to hide.

My eyes flick around the room, but there isn't anywhere I can go. Then I look to the side window in the kitchen area and the rusted fire escape landing just outside it.

Darting across the floor, I move as fast as possible over the carpet until I'm facing the window. The keys are in Victor's hands again, and I can hear them being pushed into the lock.

Seconds. I have seconds.

I grip hard to the windowsill as a sudden thought flashes through my mind—are these painted over too?

Panic sends my mind into overdrive, but the feeling of the window moving pulls me back in.

It opens about a foot before stopping. It won't budge anymore. I have no time.

My ribs scream when I lie across the rough windowsill, the various wood and metal pieces jutting into me as I force myself through the gap.

The door swings open.

He's coming.

Light filters into the apartment from the hallway bulb, making me feel like I'm on fire.

Get through. Just get through.

I force myself out, my right foot finding purchase on the rickety landing before I bring the rest of me through the gap.

No sooner have I done it than the light turns on in the apartment, a blaze that sends white spots dancing across my eyes as I yank my head down, skull pounding.

Did he see me?

The window is still open. Footsteps. At any moment, I expect to hear his deep voice and look up to find his eyes staring down at me.

It's absolutely frigid out here. Pressed up against the cold brick, I've got no cover from the blasting wind that makes me shake even harder than I already am.

The fire escape creaks dangerously beneath me, sending new spikes of panic rocketing through me.

Did he hear that?

I can't move. Even a muscle twitch might make more noise, so I remain huddled with my cheek against the brick, eyes shut tight as the night wind threatens to blow me right off the metal structure.

A door thuds from inside. Bathroom door.

I chance a peek, slowly raising my eyes until I'm level with the windowsill. In the light, his apartment looks much less sinister—but I know the truth.

Victor is nowhere to be seen, which means he is in the

bathroom. With the window open, I can just catch the sound of his footsteps as he moves around inside it.

I need to shut the window. My fingers come up, looking nearly blue in the frigid night air as I press down on the window's outer fram.

For a moment it remains stuck, my heart nearly popping out of my chest. Then it begins to lower again, letting out a little hiss I pray Victor is too occupied to hear.

It shuts. Now I'm sealed off entirely.

I hunker back down against the brick, the scratchy exterior catching at the fabric of my clothes. A look down over the side nearly makes me vomit as the wind rattles the fire escape.

I'm precariously perched far off the ground with the alley beneath me. I can make out the shiny black plastic of trash bags far below me.

To my right is the street, which is where the other two windows in Victor's apartment look out. Now that I'm outside, I can hear the distant honks of traffic. It sounds almost otherworldly as I wrap my arms around myself and try to decide what to do next.

Another gust rattles the fire escape again, freezing me. It feels like this thing is made out of brittle bone, it's so rusted. If it breaks, there's nothing I could grab hold of to break the fall. Across from me is the same brick wall I can see from my own apartment.

The door swings open inside, making my breath catch in my throat. More footsteps as Victor makes his way into the main room of his apartment. There's probably no more than a couple feet of structural material separating us right now.

I don't dare breathe as I remain hunched against the exterior, cheek flush to the rough brick. The little bits of grit pressing into my flesh keep me grounded and don't allow me to spiral into absolute hysteria.

I hear a cabinet swing open and then clap shut again. Suddenly a new noise fills the air—he's turned on the TV.

I glance down at my feet again, my toes curled to keep my Crocs on my feet. Between the metal slats that sway in the breeze, I can just make out the thin ladder that leads down to the next level.

With the noise from the television distracting him, I might be able to make my way down. If I can get to the alleyway, I can circle around to the front of the building and let myself back in before racing back up to my room and slipping inside. The noise from my nocturnal neighbor will obscure the sound of my door opening and closing.

It's the only way.

I shift my leg, the tendons crying out from having been stuffed in such an uncomfortable position. The fire escape rattles again, freezing me as my eyes shift up to the bright window overhead.

Victor doesn't come to investigate. I need to move. Not just because of the chance of Victor seeing me—I really might freeze to death out here without proper clothing.

Every second my fingers get more numb, which will make my journey down even more challenging. I can't afford to waste any more time.

The ladder consists of five steps, each a metal bar that is only a couple inches wide. I put down a Croc on the first, hesitant to place all of my weight against it should it snap in half.

By some miracle, it manages to hold. In a flash I'm moving down it, my chin still tucked into my chest so that I don't actually appear in the window if Victor were to look outside.

All I can do is hope that the TV is loud enough to mask the sounds of my movements.

Bits of rust give way beneath me, the brown chips disappearing as they flutter down into the darkness. The fire escape rattles and creaks beneath my weight, further heightening my screaming desire to get down as fast as humanly possible.

I'm at the second floor level now, breathing heavily as I keep myself plastered against the brick so as not to be seen in the window.

The light is on inside, which means someone is home. I crouch down and crawl on my hands and knees to pass beneath the window before reaching the next ladder. The first bar of this one is completely rusted through.

The two pieces wiggle slightly as the wind crashes into me again. It passes right through my hoodie like it isn't even there. My head continues to pound—a cold headache that makes it hard to focus on what I need to do.

The tips of my fingers feel like ice, like they aren't even attached to me. They're stained brown from the rust now, too. Curling my fists into balls, I suck in a breath and prepare to lower myself down to the next step on the ladder.

It's a stretch, but I'm just able to get my toe against it. A dangerous crack splits the air, followed by a metallic groan as my weight comes down full on the bar. In a flash I'm down on the first level landing, pulse pounding.

The ground is still probably ten or so feet below me. It's asphalt, which wouldn't have made for a nice landing.

There's another ladder under the slats of the first-floor landing platform, but it doesn't extend all the way to the ground.

I'm guessing that's to prevent someone on the ground from climbing up the fire escape, but right now I don't care about safety regulations. There's no light in the first floor room I'm standing outside of, so I move quickly to the other side of the landing and go for the ladder.

This one has only three rungs. I make my way down them until both my feet rest on the final rung. The bar presses into the balls of my feet, making them burn as my teeth chatter.

My hands feel wooden. I can hardly reach down and close

them around the bar, but somehow I manage it.

Once I've done that, I pull out my feet and allow them to dangle like some sort of gymnast. It's still a long drop down, but I've got no other choice. Hanging here, the wind billows into me without mercy, waving me about like a flag.

I can't feel my hands. And then I'm dropping, only in the air a moment before landing hard on the pavement below. My knees buckle instantly as I careen into the brick beside me, crashing into it then sliding down and coming to a rest on the pile of trash bags.

My chest heaves as I stare up at the bottom ladder that still rattles slightly from my dismount. The smell of the trash bags is what finally forces me upright again, despite the crying of my muscles in rebellion.

Luckily, I don't seem to have hurt myself in the final drop, aside from a scraped palm. Probably the result of sliding down the face of the bricks.

I take a few uneven steps, moving as quickly as I can manage as I hunch inward to protect myself from the wind. My head continues to pound as I go, the pressure unrelenting against my temples and making my mind ache.

There's the street. I've never been so happy to see parked cars, graffiti and plastic bags blowing in the wind. Only a gate separates me from them. And that's my next dilemma—I have to get *out* to get back into my building.

Coming up against the gate, I find that it's locked. A quick jerk of the bars tells me it won't budge, which means I've got to expend more energy and climb over it.

The adrenaline from earlier is rapidly fading, leaving me feeling like a husk of a human as I grip tight to the freezing metal bars with my clumsy, wooden hands and grunt my way to the top.

The tops of the bars roll outward to prevent someone from trying this from the other side. The metal is cold and harsh, and I just want to be warm again.

Throwing myself over the other side, I come down with a clatter against the front of the gate. The impact knocks the wind from my lungs as my chest slams into the bars, and my fingers lose their grip. I drop the final couple feet to the pavement.

Gasping for air, I throw a quick look up at the third floor, where Victor's light is still on. If he were to look out his window right now, he'd see me on the street.

Hurriedly I stuff my frozen hands into my pockets and am vaguely aware of the sensation of the key against my fingertips. Pulling it out, I race back up to the front gate and pull it open.

Next is the front door, which thankfully comes unlocked in a second. The blast of heat that smashes into me as I step inside the building is the best thing I've ever felt in my life.

I waste no time racing down the length of the hallway and rushing back up the stairs, taking them two at a time.

I round the final staircase to the third floor, hearing the television blasting away. My pace slows a little when I reach the top of the staircase, my breathing ragged as I dart a look around.

Victor isn't out here. He isn't waiting for me.

In a moment I'm back in front of my door and opening it to slip into the protective darkness. I ease the door shut, allowing it to make only a small click that is swallowed instantly by the noise from next door.

Only once the deadbolt is thrown do I finally let my shoulders sink and begin to process what I saw in Victor's apartment.

The cuffs on the wall are all I can see in my mind. The dull metal mounted there, waiting.

I'm not crazy like Claire thought. I've *got* to tell her what I've found.

Her life depends on it.

CHAPTER 28

My body desperately needs to sleep, but I know that's impossible.

I can't stop pacing back and forth in my room, thinking everything over.

Does Victor know?

He hasn't come sprinting out of his room to pound on my door, so as each minute passes without the sound of his door opening, I allow myself to breathe a little easier. I need to pull myself together enough to figure out my next move.

Should I call the police?

Having a secret room isn't a crime. I didn't see any blood or anything in there—another testament to how careful Victor is.

Is the presence of cuffs enough to arrest him?

If it isn't, there's no telling what he'll do to me.

Not to mention the fact that I'd have to explain how I found the secret room in the first place. That would necessitate me describing how I broke into his apartment illegally. My stomach turns at that.

Somehow, I know that Victor would be able to explain it away, and I'd be the one leaving in handcuffs.

That doesn't mean I can't still tell Claire, though. I've decided to leave an anonymous note at her address, containing the pictures.

As I pace, I hear something. That's a door opening.

My entire soul freezes as I wait with bated breath. Is it Victor?

With the television playing loudly next door, I can't zero in on exactly where it's coming from. A moment later however, I hear the click of the door again.

Whoever it was has gone back inside, allowing me to move freely once again. I step silently down my hallway, wondering who it could've been.

All my thoughts freeze like ice in my mind as something catches my eye just inside the door. It's been pushed through the slim crack at the bottom.

I stare downward, my world collapsing.

It's one of my shoe charms, a smiling pumpkin face.

It being here means only one thing.

Victor knows.

CHAPTER 29

I can't eat, I can't drink.

I can't even blink.

Victor knows.

One of my shoe charms came off my Crocs while I was inside the apartment—probably while I was forcing myself out the window.

I don't know what to do.

The message he sent by returning the charm is clear.

I know what you did.

What isn't clear is what he'll do next.

Will he call the police? I wring my hands together as my stomach flips, a wave of nausea washing over me at the thought.

No, he wouldn't. Just as I don't want the police looking into me, I'll bet he doesn't want any extra attention, either. I hope.

Lying down in my bed, I can't pull my eyes away from the dark windows beside me. I keep expecting that at any moment, I'll see red and blue lights dancing across the brick.

I don't know why he didn't pound at my door or shout. Somehow, just leaving the charm is even more scary.

Maybe that's what he was going for. He wants me to know that he knows. He wants me to feel afraid.

Well, it's working. I'm huddled in the fetal position in bed, rocking back and forth and trying not to vomit as my splintered mind tries to piece together what happens next.

I don't think I can ever go outside again. He'll be watching, waiting for me.

I've got enough groceries for two weeks.

Turning over, I force my face down into my pillow.

Why did I do that? Why did I break into his apartment? Both of us know he has me now.

If there *was* anything incriminating that remained in the secret room, I've got no doubt he's already scrubbed it clean by now. Even if I were to call the cops, they'd find nothing but a man who likes to get a little kinky.

My brain starts to burn from the lack of oxygen as I remain face-down in the pillow. I can't believe I was so careless.

It's taken me years to finally pull myself together after Mom. Just when I'd finally started to get things back on track…

I roll to the side and suck in a rush of oxygen, my lungs gasping hungrily for more. My hands come up to cover my face as I roll onto my back in the bed.

The only thing that keeps me from going over the edge is thinking of Claire. How I've got to warn her.

It might be too late for me, but I *will* save that girl. She doesn't deserve whatever horrible fate Victor no doubt has planned for her. My phone buzzes beside me, jarring me.

It's Derek calling, yet again.

I turn on *Do Not Disturb* mode and drop my phone back down to the sheets.

I don't even have the brainspace to deal with Derek right now.

It's past one a.m., but there's absolutely no chance of me sleeping.

Victor's message still rings loud and clear in my mind. As the hours drag on, the knot in my stomach lessens slightly.

It seems I was right—Victor doesn't want to call the police. That at least is something, though not nearly enough. The stress of everything else is a boulder that drags my spirits down with it.

This battle I've found myself in is not one I'm prepared to fight. My thoughts again return to Claire.

All I need to do is warn her. Warn her, and I'll be satisfied. My hands move to my phone again, the glow burning my eyeballs as I pull up her social media.

She posted pics from an evening wine get together with her girlfriends, all of them leaning in with their glasses raised. The table setting is filled with faux fall foliage, the leaves scattered across the tabletop.

I bite my nail as my eyes flick over the image, the bright screen burning into my retinas.

The wind presses hard against my windows, bringing my attention to them. I shiver despite the warmth in the apartment as I think of my time out on the landing.

My head still pounds. Shakily I manage to push myself off the bed and pad up to the fridge, where I pull out my water filter and pour myself a glass of water.

There isn't much left in the filter, meaning I have to refill it from the sink. Even the idea of doing that seems impossible right now, so I don't. I'm just so exhausted, mentally and physically.

My palm stings from where it slammed into the brick. I cup the glass between my hands, the cold liquid sliding down my dry throat and fluttering across my chest.

Once I've drunk my fill, I set the glass down and go back to bed.

The television next door lets off a round of gunshots, the

barely-muffled pops hardly even jarring me as I slip beneath the covers.

Somehow I manage to drift off, even without my headphones.

———

My eyes snap open the next morning as I push myself upright. Light comes in through the foggy windows, dull due to the season.

I still have a distant headache that makes me wince as I rub my eyes. My stomach grumbles for the first time in what feels like days.

After using the bathroom, I dig through the pantry and pull out some crackers. Pairing that with deli meat and slices of cheese, I've got mini sandwiches. I peck at them like a bird while I run through the events of last night again in my mind.

I feel numb.

Once the food is consumed, I stare blankly at my laptop screen. There's work to be done for the law firm, but I can't get myself to even open it.

My thoughts keep drifting back to Claire, and my promise to get the information to her. The problem now is that to do so, I have to leave my apartment. I don't have a printer here, which means I'll have to go to the library or an office store to print out the images so I can put them in the envelope.

The alternative is reaching out over social media, but I'm worried if she knows it's from me, she'll think I made it all up.

That means I've got to step foot outside the apartment. It's a struggle just to pull my trench coat over my sweatshirt, my arms feeling like they weigh a thousand pounds.

What if he's waiting for me?

As terrifying as that thought is, my desire to get this information to Claire somehow outweighs it.

It fills me with enough strength to pull on my trusty Crocs, even as my fingers tremble a little.

I'm just about to start walking down the hallway when I look back to the kitchen counter. I've got a knife in one of the drawers. If Victor tries something on the way back, at least I'll have that to defend myself.

It's not much, more for peace of mind than anything else. I stuff the knife into the deep pocket of my trench coat and grab my keys.

It's quiet as I approach the door, moving as silently as I can.

With no television, the hall is hushed. Dropping my eye to the peephole, I give the hall a once-over.

All clear.

Carefully I undo the deadbolt and then bring my door open—only to lock eyes with Victor, who has done the same on the other side.

He *was* watching me.

Now he's walking right toward me.

CHAPTER 30

I slam the door shut and slam the deadbolt into place. Victor's fist pounds against the wood a second later.

"Salem," he hisses through the frame.

I stagger backwards, drawing the knife from my pocket in a shaking hand.

"We need to talk," he says.

My head begins to shake a vehement refusal, even though he can't see me. I know that "talk" will end up with me handcuffed behind the faux wall in his apartment. I'll never be seen again.

"Stay away from me," I manage, my voice coming out stronger than I anticipated.

It's a welcome surprise, and fills me with a little more courage as I grip tighter to the knife.

"I know what you are," I say.

"You don't understand," Victor responds in a hushed tone, "I have no control. We need–"

A sudden shrill ring cuts him off. I blink.

It's a phone. He's getting a phone call.

"Hey Claire," he says, his tone completely changed.

It sounds pleasant and airy as he speaks to her. My blood runs cold.

I have no control.

"Sure, I'm here. Text me when you're outside my door."

Oh my God. Victor just admitted to me he has no control, and now Claire is going to step into his apartment.

It's the last thing I hear before his door slams shut again. Claire is coming *here.*

My mind races as the adrenaline courses through my veins from our confrontation. This could be my chance to warn her—but will she even believe me?

I have to try. Her very life may depend on it. Racing back into my apartment, I plaster myself against the glass of the window to get a view of the street at the end of the alley.

There—a flash of blonde hair as Claire passes by. She'll be at the front door in moments.

Now is my chance, and I have to take it. I've got the pictures I took last night on my phone.

It has to be enough. I have to convince her they're real. I can't let her go into that apartment again.

I'm a jumble of nerves as I move back to the hallway again, my trench coat and sneakers still on.

Save Claire.

That's the only thing I'm thinking. *Save Claire.*

I don't know if Victor is about to snap or what, but I'm not taking any chances. I throw open my door and shoot across the hall to the stairs, practically flying down them in a race to the first floor.

I can hear Claire coming inside, the front door closing and cutting off the sounds of the city. My feet come down on the second floor landing and then I'm rounding the corner and taking the next flight of stairs.

Claire looks up in surprise as I scramble into the main hallway, her hands clutching tightly to her phone at the sudden burst of movement.

Once the shock is gone however, I see the recognition in her eyes, followed by a slight recoil as her mouth opens.

I don't let her speak.

"You have to listen to me," I say, swallowing around ragged breaths as I fumble for my phone.

"Please. I know it sounds utterly insane, but I have proof, I swear. Victor is dangerous."

Claire blinks, her mouth still hanging open for another second before she closes it and crosses her arms.

"What proof?"

I feel a glimmer of hope. She's giving me a chance, and that's all I need. Hurriedly I unlock my phone and tap over to the photos.

The images of the cuffs on the brick wall as well as shots of the enclosed space appear on my screen.

I flip it around to show her, heart pounding.

"I found a secret room in Victor's apartment—with hand-cuffs," I say.

Claire squints a little, and then her eyes widen as she realizes what she's looking at.

"What?"

I nod. "It's behind the couch in his apartment. Claire, I think he's been hiding bodies in there. Bodies of girls."

Claire's face has gone a shade paler, her lips pursed as she flicks her large eyes up at my face. She's probably trying to decide if I'm nuts, or if she should listen to me.

"This… room is in Vic's place?"

I nod again.

"How did—"

My hand comes up to stop her. "Please, don't ask. Just listen to what I'm saying. Victor has threatened me multiple times, and I think he's going to hurt you too. You've got to stay away."

To my surprise, Claire's eyebrows pinch together in a look of anger, not fear. She crosses her arms again, too.

"Stay away? Are you kidding me? I want an explanation."

"F—from him?" I sputter.

"Absolutely. I want to look him in the eyes and show him these photos. That'll tell me everything I need to know," she says.

She's much stronger than I am.

"But what if he—"

Claire looks over at me, her eyes fiery. "He tries anything? I wish he would."

She opens her purse, revealing a tiny black handgun stuffed inside. It's the smallest gun I've ever seen, but it's clear from her expression it's no toy.

I blink, staring at it as she flashes me a smile.

"It's New York City. Nothing scares away creeps like a glock," she says with a wink.

I can't believe how brave she is. Before I know it, Claire is moving toward the staircase. She glances over her shoulder at me, her blonde hair falling across her back.

"Are you coming?"

"You… you want me to?" I ask.

"I talk a good game, but Victor is a big guy. If both of us are there, I don't think he'd try anything," Claire says with a grin.

Taking a breath, I smooth my hands along my trench coat.

"Okay," I say finally.

"Then let's do this. I want some answers," Claire says, setting her jaw.

We move quickly up the stairs, my heart in my throat the whole time. What is Victor going to say when we confront him?

I want to have the cops on speed-dial, just in case this gets really crazy. Claire does have the gun, though.

The question is, what weapons does Victor have?

So many thoughts fly through my brain it's impossible to

think straight. Before I know it we're on the second floor landing and rounding to walk up to the third.

In a few seconds, everything will be out on the table.

We get to the third floor, and I can hardly breathe. Claire marches right up to Victor's door, seeming completely undeterred.

I admire her gumption, but hope it doesn't backfire. If she comes in with too much heat, Victor might snap.

I think about mentioning Victor's words to me, but by the time I do it's already too late.

Claire's pounding on the door.

"Victor," she calls out. "I've got some questions for you."

CHAPTER 31

I can hear Victor's footsteps on the other side of the door.

He's going to open it, and then who knows what happens next. I can hardly think straight as I hear the door being unlocked.

It swings inward to reveal Victor's large frame.

He's got a light smile on his face, but it falters as his eyes move past Claire and settle on me.

"What's—"

"Inside," Claire says.

The word comes out sharp. It's not a suggestion, it's a command.

To my surprise, Victor obeys and moves away from the doorway to allow us entry.

Claire walks right in, her boots clacking loudly on the old wooden floor. I scamper inside behind her, sticking close to her side as if that'll protect me from Victor.

Claire reaches the main room and whirls around to Victor, who's gone pale.

Does he know she knows?

I can tell from his expression that something is definitely wrong.

"Claire," he says.

Claire shakes her head. She hasn't pulled out the gun yet. Victor doesn't look like he's going to attack us at all—more like he might pass out himself.

Maybe he knows the gig is up.

I dart my eyes over at Claire, who strangely enough is smiling. She's even more courageous than I'd thought, if she can face down Victor with a smile.

He's backed against the kitchen counter. I can see beads of sweat dripping down the sides of his temples. He looks skittish almost, his Adam's apple rising and falling as he swallows.

"She doesn't know," Victor says.

My brow furrows. Is he talking about me? I definitely *do* know.

Suddenly the gun is up, emerging from Claire's purse in a flash.

My heartbeat quickens. This is it.

"You're lying to me, Victor. She just showed me pictures," Claire says.

I blink.

What is this conversation?

My mind is racing so fast I can hardly comprehend the words I'm hearing. Victor is shaking his head.

Then his eyes settle on me.

"I'm sorry," he says in a quiet voice.

Sorry for what?

Then Claire turns, still grinning. Only now, the pistol is pointed at *me*.

"Should've minded your own business, Salem," she says sweetly as she cocks the hammer back.

CHAPTER 32

Victor

I warned Salem she should've minded her own business, but she didn't listen.

All she had to do was keep her head down, and not ask questions. Now, Claire's going to do something awful to her —the same thing that was done to me.

My heart thuds against my sternum as I see the color drain from Salem's face. It's obvious she's confused at the sudden turn of events.

So was I, all those years ago when Claire revealed her true self to me.

"What's going on?" Salem asks in a small voice, her body pressed against the wall.

I want to go to her, defend her. But I know if I move, Anya will pay for it.

Claire's smile only widens at Salem's confusion.

"I know all about the secret room, sweetie. I'm the one who put it in," she says, her voice still dripping with that false sweetness that makes my skin crawl.

She turns back to me, waving the pistol in my direction and making me stiffen.

"Where do you think I put Victor when he's been a bad boy?"

My heart hammers in my chest at the thought of being locked inside that cell again. The walls are sound-proofed. No one can hear me shout, no matter how loudly I yell.

The first few times she locked me in, I shouted until my throat was raw. It didn't help. No one came. No one heard me.

The first time she locked me in, it was because I'd tried to escape the apartment. It only took two, three-day sessions of no food and water, completely alone in the darkness, to dispel that idea from my mind.

Besides, Claire has Anya. Anything I try, she punishes Anya for it.

Salem looks as if she's about to cry. "I don't understand," she says.

Claire rolls her gorgeous blue eyes in a mocking gesture. "Obviously. That's the point. I don't want the whole world to know what I'm up to, do I?"

Salem swallows quickly, her eyes darting over to me. I stare back at her, but there's nothing to say.

It's all out in the open now. Now that Salem knows part of the truth, I know what's going to happen.

She'll be a prisoner here, like me. Like the rest of us. *None of us can ever leave.*

"W—what *are* you doing?" Salem asks.

"Why doesn't big, handsome Vic tell her?" Claire asks in a sickly sweet tone.

It's lovey-dovey, but there's absolutely no love behind it. I know the true Claire—if that's even this monster's real name.

I doubt any of her friends know what I know.

My jaw remains clenched, unwilling to reveal the last bit of truth to Salem. Even though I know it's too late, I don't want to be the one who has to tell her. Who has to explain why she can never leave this apartment again.

Claire is going to make me, though. Her bright blue eyes narrow in a silent order.

I can tell by her face she's enjoying this. She gets off on the suffering of others.

My suffering most of all—like when she makes me get with those prostitutes she sends over, watching the entire thing on the camera hidden in the dresser.

She knows what Anya means to me. We were going to be married. Now I've been forced to cheat on her so many times I've lost track.

That doesn't stop me from weeping after every encounter, though. It breaks my heart, but I know if I don't do what Claire commands, she'll punish Anya even more than she already does.

Claire waggles the gun at me again.

"Go ahead, Vicky-bear. Tell Salem here what goes on," she says, flashing her perfect teeth.

I take a shaking breath and glance over at Salem. I'm unable to meet her eyes. I can't watch another person break before me, watch the hope drain from their eyes to be replaced by utter despair.

"We... make pills. In the basement. Everyone here, we... work for Claire," I manage.

Claire smiles even wider. This is her favorite part. "And?"

"And... I take the finished product and hide it in meat before putting it in the trash."

A look of understanding flashes across Salem's face a moment before it's replaced by complete bewilderment again.

"Because who wants to dig through stinky trash?" Claire says, wrinkling her perfect button nose.

She turns the gun back to Salem.

"It's a good thing you're so nosy, actually. Production has been... lacking recently. I've been looking for a fresh pair of hands."

I shudder as I think of Agatha, the older woman from the

second floor. She had arthritis in her fingers, and wasn't able to work as fast as the rest of us. That put her on Claire's radar.

Then Agatha made the mistake of trying to warn Salem when she first moved in. When Claire found out, she locked Agatha in the secret cell in her room.

That was days ago, and I haven't seen her since.

Salem's head is shaking now, her entire body trembling in fear.

"Please…" she says.

Claire cocks her head.

"I thought—please, just let me go," Salem pleads.

"Oh sweetie," Claire says with a click of her tongue. "From the moment you signed the lease, I was never going to let you go."

Claire owns the entire building. I didn't know it either, when I first signed on. I was just excited to have a studio of my own, and for a cheap enough rate that I could overlook the dilapidated state of the place and less-than-stellar amenities.

It took less than a month before Claire owned me. I thought I was just making friends with a nice girl across the hall—then she showed her true colors when I mentioned Anya coming to visit.

She wanted me all to herself.

Once Claire locked up Anya too, I was totally powerless. She knew how much I loved Anya, how I'd do anything for her.

The next few years were a nightmare. If I acted in a way Claire deemed unsatisfactory while pretending to be her boyfriend, she'd put me in the box. Twice, she even conjured up domestic assault charges against me, literally punching herself in the face to blacken her eye while telling me no one would believe my side.

She was right.

I never ended up doing time, because Claire insisted she

didn't want to press charges. To the world, she looked every bit the battered girlfriend who refused to see the dark side of her abusive boyfriend.

I knew the truth. All of it was a threat. A warning.

A warning that if I kept acting up, she could have me thrown into prison at any time.

Life has been a true nightmare for the past four years. It feels like much, much longer. Every day I exist is filled with torment. Now that will be Salem's life, too.

Claire is smart. Brutally smart. She knows exactly who to let into the building.

New hires, she calls them. She does extensive background checks and learns everything she can about the person.

She only picks those without many close friends or relatives. No locals live here, only outcasts and introverts who wouldn't be noticed if they went missing. Nearly nine million people live in this city.

All of us living in this building could disappear and no one would be wiser. Grains of sand in a vast ocean.

I grit my teeth, my armpits drenched in sweat.

I really tried to scare Salem into staying away. Tried my hardest.

It didn't do any good.

Something bad is going to happen to Salem now, and there's nothing I can do to stop it.

CHAPTER 33

can't think straight.

All of this is too insane. It's the truth though–I can tell that much from Victor's pained expression.

I had it completely backwards. All of it. Victor isn't the bad guy, Claire is. Always has been. I swallow around the massive lump in my throat, feeling weak in the knees as Claire's gaze bounces between the two of us.

She has a little pouty expression on her face.

"What's wrong, Vic? Sad to see another one? You should be, I suppose. Maybe if you hadn't been so careless, she would've had another month or two of freedom."

Her harsh words, delivered in such a sweet voice, are jarring and scare me almost as much as the gun.

This whole time, Victor wasn't trying to kill me. He was trying to *protect* me.

Pieces of the puzzle click into position in my brain, each of them striking me like a punch. The blood on his shirt must've been from his shifts stuffing the pills into the meat.

I swallow hard again, thinking of the bloody trash bag. It hadn't contained a body after all, and Victor hadn't lied to the police. It really was filled with meat, only the police weren't made aware of what was *in* that meat.

Victor's words echo through my mind again.

Mind your own business. You won't like what happens to you if you don't.

It wasn't a threat. It was a warning. He was trying to help me.

He couldn't tell me the truth, not with the amount of cameras Claire has set up all throughout the building.

All of it is too much. The realizations continue to rock through me as Claire takes a step toward me, her chic boots clopping across the wood floors.

"You'll start in the basement soon enough. You definitely have some spirit—I bet you'll be a very productive worker," she says.

Pills. This whole thing is about pills.

I suppress the urge to vomit as I think about the empty, distant looks I got from the other neighbors I've seen. All of them are Claire's prisoners, forced to work all day before returning to be locked into their prison-cell studio apartments at night.

Now I understand why I hardly saw anyone. No one is free to leave, and I'll bet Claire has a way of locking and unlocking the apartments remotely, like she can do with the front door.

It hadn't been a malfunction at all, that day the door wouldn't open. My vision blurs as the reality of my situation hits me.

That door is going to remain locked.

I can't leave.

Glancing back over at Victor, I can see the pain on his face. How long has he been Claire's prisoner?

I think of the two assault arrests, my blood running cold. Claire. All of it was Claire.

Those took place years ago, which means Victor has been here a long, long time.

Claire turns back to Victor and flicks the gun to the right.

"You've been a bad boy again, Vic. Allowing the police to show up here is a big, big no-no. Not to mention all those silly, misguided attempts to tell Salem here the truth."

Suddenly the sweetness drops from Claire's voice as she speaks again, and I get a sense of her true personality.

"Get in the box," she hisses.

Victor pales a little, but slowly walks over to the couch before pushing it to the side. He presses on the secret door and manages to fold his massive body inside. Claire follows him, her voice a low murmur I can't make out as the handcuffs clack shut.

She steps back out and smooths her jacket before tilting her head slightly to speak to Victor with one hand propped on the secret door.

"You know, I think I'll pay a visit across the hall, too. Anya needs to be made aware of all this unacceptable behavior."

"Claire please don't," Victor pleads.

His voice is desperate.

It only makes Claire's smile widen as she begins to shut the door.

"Your little girlfriend hates you now, you know that? She's said it to me herself, in the brief moments I remove the tape and turn the TV down."

Oh my god. Understanding slaps me across the face as Claire's words finally reach me.

Paying a visit across the hall. She's talking about my next-door neighbor, whom I took to be some sort of inconsiderate night owl.

That's not the case at all— it's not some jerk. It's Victor's girlfriend, Anya.

She's being tortured in there, forced to stay awake watching a painfully loud television set for hours on end.

My heart breaks as I think back to my pounding against the wall, all the anger and indignation I felt.

How little I knew. Anya was probably in there screaming for help, and here I was smacking the wall to get her to shut up.

I can't breathe. All of this is too much, too awful.

"Leave Anya alone," Victor continues to beg. "Punish me, not her. Please Claire, I—"

Victor's pleading is cut off as the secret door clicks shut. It's horrifying how the grown man's yelling is now utterly absent. Even straining my hearing, I can't hear a thing.

Claire turns back toward me now, her bright smile sending spikes of anxiety shooting through me. There's a look in her eyes that sets my mind reeling.

She's truly evil.

And she's looking right at me.

"Now that he's been dealt with, it's time to decide what to do about you," she says, tapping the pistol against her lips.

I'm pinned against the wall. There's nowhere to run, nowhere to hide. The front door is locked. The windows are painted shut.

The only one that isn't is the one in Victor's kitchen, which I now understand is because he was supposed to drop the pill-containing trash bags out the window and onto the pile of bags below.

When I left through the fire escape, I should've just run and not looked back. I should've left my meager belongings behind, because now I'm trapped here with a psychopath.

Claire nods, seeming to savor my growing horror.

"There's no box in your room—yet. Still renovating the building, you know? But you'll spend the next few days locked in the apartment, I think. Enough time for you to understand."

Understand what?

I can't think too hard on that, because she's coming right toward me. Claire's heels strike the floor as she raises the gun.

The black hole of its barrel points right at me, freezing me against the wall as my chest tightens. She's not going to shoot me is she?

Then something smashes into my head, and everything goes dark.

CHAPTER 34

The world swims around me.

My eyelids flutter as I start to lift my head, only to wince and hiss at the explosion of pain that rocks my body. It feels like my skull is cracked. Maybe it is.

I lift a hand to touch my aching head, only to find that I can't—I'm handcuffed to something. The harsh metal cuts into my wrist, and my hand has already begun to change colors.

I blink at the blindingly white light that glares down at me from above.

Where am I?

There's movement in front of me. I blink again, clearing my vision a little more. Claire stares back at me, her golden hair falling across her shoulder.

"There she is," she says.

I can't speak. My head hurts too much. It feels like there's a boulder-sized welt on my head. Each breath makes it pulse, sending another shockwave of pain through me.

It makes it hard to focus on Claire and comprehend what she's saying.

"—figure two or three days should be enough," she

finishes.

I blink at her again, my eyes brimming with tears. The handcuff chain jingles as I shift position while trying not to throw up. I'm attached to a pipe that runs behind the toilet in my own bathroom.

"You'll figure out how things work around here soon enough, I expect. You're a smart girl," Claire says with a smile.

Her teeth are perfect. It's all a disguise for the rotten horror that lies beneath.

She pulls out her phone again, and holds it up in front of me.

"What are you doing?" I mumble, my words coming out slightly slurred.

Claire leans to the side so she can see me around her phone. "Taking a photo. For the memories, of course. Now hush."

There's a click as her phone takes a picture of me huddled into the tiny space beside the toilet. Spiderwebs and dead insects litter the cold tile around me. I see splotches of blood, too.

Claire pulls her hands back, her pretty eyes taking in the photo. She shakes her head, letting out a little cluck before she holds the phone back up.

"That one's no good. Can't see your eyes. Camera's up here, sweetie."

I snap my head up even though the sudden movement nearly makes me hurl.

"Screw you," I hiss, spit bubbling out of my mouth and splattering the chipped tile in front of me.

Another click.

"That's much better," Claire says with that same sickening smile plastered across her face.

This woman is truly deranged. You'd never know it by looking at her, though I suppose that's the point.

She's a wolf hiding in plain sight. So innocent and normal-looking, just another girl in the city. I'm ashamed to say I fell for it hook, line, and sinker.

Now I'm paying the price.

Claire checks out the new photo and then gives a satisfied nod. "That's it, then. I'm sure you're feeling a lot of things right now, so I'll leave you to it. Be back to check on you in a couple days."

A couple days? My stomach churns at the thought of being stuck in this position for that long.

"By the way, you should know I emailed your boss at the law firm and gave them your resignation. Taking some time to yourself," Claire says with a giggle.

She takes a step closer to me, keenly aware of exactly how much range of motion I have while cuffed to the pipe. Claire squats down, the fabric of her jacket making a little swish noise in the tight space.

Our faces are level now. I stare at her, my head pounding and eyes blurry with tears.

Everything hurts.

Claire flicks her eyes over my face with a nod.

"You need to understand this is your life now," she says in a soft voice.

My mouth hangs open as I breathe heavily, able to do little more than watch and listen.

Claire tongues the inside of her lip. "You'll get it soon enough, I expect. Everyone always does."

She rises, cheerful once again, the peppy tone the total opposite of how I feel. With that, she turns on a bootheel and starts toward the bathroom door.

"Why are you doing this?" I manage with a wince.

Even speaking makes my body tremble with pain. The reverberations of my words bounce around my skull, the wound on my head screaming in agony.

Claire pauses with her hand on the doorknob. The bright

smile is still plastered across her face, but I can see now what a mask it truly is. She looks over her shoulder, her twinkling eyes meeting my gaze.

"Because I can," she says.

The simplicity of the statement is the most terrifying thing of all. Claire is a monster.

My head drops back down as exhaustion racks my body.

"Now be good, and maybe I'll consider raising the toilet's water level enough so you can drink it."

I hear the door shut but hardly have the strength to open my eyes.

Claire's boots click across the boards, and then the front door opens with a creak.

It slams shut a second later, leaving only silence. Chained to the pipe, all I can hear is my own ragged breathing.

Even the slightest movement makes my head spin. I don't know what to do, what to think.

All of this is so unbelievable, and yet here I am.

Two weeks ago, I was swearing up and down I'd move into any apartment that would have me. What a mistake that was.

My scattered thoughts move to Victor, who's chained up inside the hole in his wall, no one to hear his pleas for help.

Next door to me is his girlfriend, Anya. I can't even imagine what she's gone through. What all of the people here have.

A nightmare.

Darkness takes me as I slip into the abyss once again.

———

My eyes snap open.

Glancing at the tiny frosted window above the toilet, I can tell it's nighttime now, but I've no idea what day it is.

Based on the hunger burning a hole in my stomach, I can

assume I've been here a while.

My head aches, but it's not the overwhelming, nauseating sense of pain I felt earlier. With my newfound ability to turn my head, I look over myself in the harsh bathroom light.

Bloodstains coat my right shoulder. My head must've been tilted to the right against the toilet seat while I was out.

I swallow the sense of panic rising in my throat as I lift my right arm again. The handcuff around my wrist is so tight that my hand has gone numb. It's a cold bluish-purple color, looking almost half dead.

There's dried blood there, too. My lips are cracked and dry as I run my tongue over the surface of them.

Panic threatens to engulf my mind. All of this is too much. Even if I manage to get free of the handcuffs and leave the bathroom, I'm still stuck in the apartment. No doubt Claire has locked my door from the outside.

There's no way to escape. Nowhere to go.

Trapped in this building, forever.

Trapped in my room, like Mom used to do to me.

You've been a bad girl, Salem. Bad girls deserve to be punished.

My eyes snap shut again as I begin to hyperventilate. It's happening again. It's happening again, and there's nothing I can do to stop it.

No.

I blink hard, fighting back the tears as I try to remain somewhat level-headed.

Mom wasn't able to keep me locked up forever.

Claire no doubt knows my history of juvenile delinquency and mental hospital commitments.

It's probably why she even allowed me to move in here in the first place.

What she doesn't know—what nobody knows—is what happened *after* my last trip to the hospital.

What Dr. DeLuca and I did to Mom, so she could never abuse me again.

CHAPTER 35

I still see her face sometimes, frozen in that final scream before she fell down the stairs.

I'd just been let out of another five-day stay in my room, punishment for begging the mental hospital workers to take me seriously.

They took my rambling as a sign of whatever mental illness Mom told them I had and informed her of everything I'd said.

Over those five days, I paid for it, with interest. I could hardly move, my body was so weak from lack of food.

Each day, she pushed a small plate of water under the crack in the door. I had to lap at it like a dog, and there was never enough. It was only just enough to keep me alive.

I see the hallway in my mind, Mom in front of me as she drags me by my painfully thin wrist toward the stairs.

"Maybe now you've finally learned your lesson," she said.

My mind was so scrambled from the lack of sustenance I could barely comprehend her words. Even if I'd wanted to, I didn't have the strength to respond.

All I could think of was what Dr. DeLuca had said to me

on our final visit before I was released back into Mom's custody.

Sometimes, the best thing to do is let go... let go of the beliefs about right and wrong that society has forced you to accept.

I saw the handsome psychiatrist's face in my mind then, his kind smile as he looked at me. He really was gorgeous, and in that moment, I understood what I had to do.

As Mom reached the top of the staircase, all it took was a nudge from me. A nudge was all I could muster from my broken, drained body.

A nudge was all I needed.

I called Dr. DeLuca after it was over, told him what I'd done through waves of tears.

"You did a good thing, Salem," he told me in that calm voice of his.

I might've been delirious from dehydration and starvation, but I could've sworn I heard a hint of a smile in his voice.

The memory fades from my injured head as I blink away black spots from my vision. I'm back in present time, still in the bathroom, still chained to the pipe.

Dr. DeLuca's smirk appears in my mind as he whispers.

You can't control what other people do, only your own actions and response... so choose actions so violent no one dares mess with you again.

He was right, as usual. I can only control my own actions.

I won't allow my life to be chosen for me. Not *this* life, which is something perhaps worse than death. Victor and Anya and the other building tenants can't be left to suffer, either.

Someone has to do something.

Just as when the police and the nurses wouldn't help me with Mom, I'll have to do this on my own, too.

I tug against the handcuff, eliciting an instant burn across my wrist as the metal cuts into my skin again. Red drops of blood well up against the cuff and drip down to the dusty tile.

The pipe gives its signature rattle as I pull again, ignoring the flashing pain in my hand.

I refuse to let Claire dictate my life, just as I, eventually, refused to let Mom.

Claire might've destroyed my career, even my life, but she made one fatal mistake.

She's underestimated me. Everyone always does.

I'm small, anxious, and quick to cry.

That doesn't mean I'm helpless.

I look down at my Crocs and the bright plastic shoe charms poking out of most of the holes.

It hurts to stretch my free arm down to the shoe, but I push through the pain and pop out the skull charm.

Instead of the plastic piece that's supposed to be on the underside, there's a small bundle of metal wire and hot glue holding it in place.

I was ashamed of my cheap fix in the past, but not now. Now, that piece of wire will be the thing that saves me.

Dr. DeLuca taught me how to pick a lock, how to escape a cell—how else could we have our late-night therapy sessions?

I clasp the small skeleton charm in a trembling hand, focusing hard even though it makes my head pound.

Bringing my hands together, I'm able to unfurl the wire and rip the glued piece off the back of the charm.

It takes almost a minute, but then the handcuff emits a soft click, and my hand instantly lets out an interior sigh of relief as the blood rushes back to my cold fingers.

I'm free. I pull my wrist to my chest, my other fingers working over my numb hand to try and massage some life back into it.

My head pulses, my thoughts clouded and sticky. I think I've got a concussion.

It takes a while to get back to my feet. The world swims

more than once, but finally I'm standing upright again and bracing myself against the wall as I breathe in and out.

One staggering step toward the door. Another.

My hand comes down on the handle, my blood-stained fingers wrapping around it. I twist, and the door creaks open. My apartment is dark, barren.

Claire has taken my computer, my phone. My food.

My stomach pangs as I lean against the fridge. It hits me in waves, but there's nothing I can do.

I stumble over to the sink, but find that no water comes out of the faucet even when I twist the handles all the way.

She's cut off the water, too.

I sag against the kitchen sink basin, the crushing state of my situation threatening to overtake me completely.

Then a shrill scream rips through the air—the TV next door in Anya's room.

Now that I know it's being used as an instrument of torture, the sound doesn't make me angry at my neighbor. It makes me angry at Claire, and that fuels me enough to straighten me back upright.

I take a shaking breath and look to my right at the wall we share.

I need to get in there and help her. We may not be able to leave the building, but I know for a fact I can pick the locks on these doors.

It's what I did to get into Victor's room.

My fingers close around the small piece of wire in my grip.

I can't give up. I'm starving, but I push any thought of food out of mind.

I need to keep my mind as clear as I can. The wound on the back of my head pulses and makes it hard to focus on what I need to do next.

If I step out into the hallway and go to unlock Anya's door, Claire will see me on the hallway camera.

The gig will be up before it even begins. A siren wails from the television next door, making the thin wall tremble.

I blink. That's it.

I don't even have to pass in front of the hallway cameras at all.

Digging through my cabinets, I find that Claire has taken my dinner knives, too. She wants to leave nothing to chance.

I step back from the counter, my breathing hitched as I search for something to break through the drywall. I don't care about getting my deposit back, that's for sure.

My eyes fall to the bed frame. It's a rickety wooden thing, with peg legs about a foot high. I move over to the bed and squat down, feeling a wave of pain wash over me at the sudden change in altitude. My head definitely needs more time to heal, but I simply don't have it.

If I don't act now, I'll never be able to.

The leg comes unscrewed easily. It's some light type of wood, maybe poplar. It doesn't really matter.

Gripping the wooden block between both hands, I turn toward the shared wall again, my jaw clenched.

This is it.

I don't know what I'll find on the other side in Anya's room. Given how sadistic Claire is, it certainly won't be anything good.

My chest tightens, but I remain strong. I refuse to submit to her.

It's only a couple steps to the wall. The closer I get, the louder the television seems to blare. The surface of the drywall is cold to the touch as I run my fingers across it. The paint is chipped and stained.

Then I raise the bed frame leg, and bring it down hard.

CHAPTER 36

Dust kicks up into the air as I attack the drywall with every ounce of my strength.

My wound is screaming at me, but it only fuels me further. I know if I don't get through this wall, much worse will happen to me.

A hole appears. I'm pulling at the wall now, yanking off chunks with my fingers before tossing them to the floor.

The air is choked with white dust. I hack a cough into my sleeve and continue my onslaught.

After another few strikes, the hole is wide enough for my head to poke through. There are a few thin pieces of wood making up the skeletal frame of the wall. More drywall hits the floor.

I'm looking at the backside of Anya's wall now. The TV is so loud it makes my ears pulse in tune with the pounding across the back of my head.

I push through it, bringing my piece of wood up again before thrusting it like a spear into the wall.

The drywall begins to crack and crumble. Shouts from the show fill in the gaps.

Almost there.

Gritting my teeth, I force the bed leg through the wall again and this time, the hole is wide enough I have a glimpse of the other apartment. It's dark.

The hole widens as I pull pieces off, my fingers ghostly white with the amount of dust accumulating on them. I step into the wall itself, positioning myself between the wood supports to get better access to the second wall.

The hole in it is nearly big enough now for me to fit through. I let out a grunt as I snap off a large piece and throw it carelessly behind me.

There's a ghastly glow lighting Anya's apartment from the television.

It's also louder than I would have ever thought possible. That noise can't be coming from the TV alone, can it?

There's a smell filtering into my nostrils now that makes me gag.

With a final gasp, I push through the hole and stumble into my neighbor's apartment.

That's when I see her, and my stomach drops.

In the glow of the television, I can make out the details of the sparse apartment. There isn't much at all besides a large black leather recliner sitting less than a foot from the TV.

Positioned around it are floor-standing speakers, all of them blaring the noise at absolutely deafening levels toward Anya.

The girl is sagging against cuffs and binds that have been added to the recliner. From the look of them, she hasn't been free in a long, long time.

Her oily hair hangs in front of her face as she remains tilted forward, unmoving. There's a long, neon orange bendy straw duct taped over her mouth. My eyes follow it down to the base of the chair, where a small mountain of meal-replacement shake bottles lie, empty.

Oh my God. This is the worst thing I've ever seen.

It makes my stomach turn. I rush over to her, my heart in my throat.

Is she still alive?

She hasn't reacted in the slightest to my demolition session.

Please, don't be dead. Please.

The speakers are so deafening I can't think straight as I stagger forward. My head is pounding so hard it's literally making my vision flicker. My breath comes in heaving gasps as I grab hold of one of the speakers, my hands vibrating from the sound level emanating from it.

I toss it backwards, tipping it over.

There's movement from Anya, who wrenches her head to the side, eyes wide with pure fear.

My heart breaks even further at the sight of her full face in the light. She's deathly thin, nothing but a layer of skin draped across bones.

"Anya?" I shout to be heard over the noise from the TV.

The girl doesn't react.

I've got to turn this off. Where's the remote?

I look down at the tv stand, feeling a twinge in my chest.

The remote is inches from Anya's hand, but just out of reach. I've got absolutely no doubt Claire positioned it there on purpose to torture Anya even more.

Thoughts of being trapped like this for weeks or months flood my brain, making tears well up in my eyes as I scoop up the remote with trembling hands. I click off the television, draping a merciful blanket of silence over the apartment.

My ears continue to ring with the ghosts of the TV's sound.

Anya is so weak, she literally can't keep her head turned toward me. It sags downward again as a string of saliva falls from her lips.

The bendy straw seems to glow in the light as it flexes

with her movement. I bend down in front of her and carefully peel the duct tape from her mouth.

Anya lets out a gasp at the freedom.

"Who… are you?" she pants.

Her words come out in little more than a whisper. I can hear some sort of light Eastern European accent.

"I moved in next door."

Anya's head shakes back and forth with the slightest movement.

"I cannot… hear you," she whispers.

Her hearing has been totally destroyed by the oppressive noise level forced on her night after night. Waves of guilt crash over me as I think of all the days I sat in my room complaining about the noise.

I could've done something, if only I'd known.

My head whips back and forth as I look around the apartment. I hold up a finger to tell Anya I'll be right back and then move into the kitchen area. A search of the drawers reveals one pen, but no paper.

The bathroom. I stalk over to the bathroom and pull the door open. Flicking on the light reveals a toilet that has not been cleaned in months. It's practically a swamp now, filled with dark green and black mold that is literally growing out of the bowl. The sink is in a similar state.

I grab the roll of toilet paper off the holder and step back into the main room.

If the bathroom looks like that, that means Anya's had to…

Another shiver runs through me as I look at the poor girl. That explains the smell in here. She's been soiling herself for months. Claire is truly the worst human being I've ever encountered or even heard of.

Hurriedly I bring the roll back over to her and pull off a couple squares so I can scribble down something.

Next door neighbor, I hastily write in pen before holding it up in front of Anya.

The skeletal girl blinks in acknowledgement.

"Is Victor… okay?" she whispers, her voice cracking.

CHAPTER 37

Everything this girl has been through, and the first thing she asks is about someone else.

That warms my heart a little bit. Claire was lying to Victor when she told him Anya hated him.

Despite everything Claire has done to this girl, she didn't break her spirit. Anya is a fighter.

I squat down beside the chair, trying not to wrinkle my nose at the odor emanating from it. I've got to get her out of here.

The locks don't stand a chance against my trusty paperclip lockpick, and soon enough I have her left arm free.

As I throw off the cuff and get a full look at her arm, my heart catches in my throat.

It's so thin I can literally see the entire outline of her bones. She's been fed just enough to keep her alive, and then only barely.

A shiver runs across my back and scalp as I round the other side of the chair to work on the other arm. Anya hasn't even lifted her free arm. I don't think she can, having not used those muscles in so long.

Once both arms are free, I crouch down and get her legs

undone. After that, it's the binds around her chest that hold her upright.

It's some sort of metal cable that has buried itself in Anya's skin long ago. The sight of the dried blood and half-healed wounds make me sick again, but I keep myself together enough to get the lock holding the cable taut undone.

It clatters to the flooring with a dull thud, and then she's free.

Without the cable keeping her upright, Anya tips forward like a ragdoll, bending almost in half as she lies there.

I race back around the chair and push her upright. Her eyelids flutter as she tries to speak, her cracked lips coming together before going slack again.

She's too weak.

My eyes go back to the kitchen. From what I know of Claire, she's probably got the fridge stocked with plenty to eat. In fact, I'll bet she's probably sat and gorged herself on a large meal while making Anya watch.

As I pull open the fridge, I find that I'm half-right. Every shelf is stocked with a meal replacement shake of some kind. Claire must do her torture-shopping in bulk.

I pull out a couple bottles and shake them up before bringing them over to Anya. The crack of the seal on the cap sends her eyelids fluttering open again as I gently tilt her head back.

"Drink this," I say, even though I know she can't hear me.

Anya seems to understand regardless, and allows me to hold on to her forehead to keep her upright. Her mouth drops open, and I tilt the shake against her lips and then a little more, allowing the liquid to flow.

The first couple of gulps are weak and almost impercepti-ble, but as sustenance flows through her, I can see her begin-ning to swallow with more effort.

After two more shakes, I toss the empty bottles to the side and wipe Anya's lips with the toilet paper.

"Thank you," she whispers to me.

There are tears in her eyes, and now I'm tearing up too. The fact she's so grateful for such a meager amount of food absolutely shatters my heart.

I watch as she tries to lift her arm, the sinewy strings of muscle she has remaining straining beneath her pale skin. Her hand comes up an inch before dropping to the chair arm as she lets out an exhausted breath.

"How long have you been here?" I ask.

I'm afraid to hear the answer, but know I need to.

Anya shakes her head again. She can't hear me.

I write out the question on the toilet paper and hold it up. Her pretty brown eyes flick over the sheet a second before she swallows and runs her tongue across her lips.

"Three… years," she says.

Another chill runs through me. *Three years.* Three years spent trapped, unable to move more than a couple muscles. I don't know how she's even still alive.

It's a testament to her inner strength.

"I'm ready to be done now," she says.

It's a joke, and despite the horrifying circumstances, I can't help but let out a little laugh as the tears stream down my cheeks. With some nutrition in her stomach now, I can see that tiny spark of life in her grow brighter.

I'll bet Claire hated that the most, and it makes me even more proud of Anya. She never broke.

"We're going to get out of here," I say before remembering she'll have had no idea I spoke and write down the message to her.

"Cameras," Anya says.

She does a small gesture with her head toward the hallway.

I nod.

I write out a question, asking if she wants more food or water. This time, Anya is able to lift her trembling arm enough to point a bony finger at *water*.

I head off to the fridge again and find a couple bottles in the back. They're old, but it doesn't matter at this point. My own throat tightens at the sight of them—I haven't had anything to drink in over a day now, either.

Still, I wouldn't dare complain, not after seeing the state Anya is in. She needs this much, much more than me.

I carry the plastic water bottles back over to her and twist off the cap. She brings up her skeletal hands to grip the bottle, but she's too weak to hold it. I help her, tilting it into her mouth as she gulps down the liquid.

That definitely helped. There's more life in her eyes now as she looks around with alertness. She glances down at her hands, turning them over slowly in front of her as if just seeing the state of herself for the first time.

Anya is definitely beautiful. There's no denying that, even in her current state. With proper nutrition, a haircut, and a skincare routine that actually allows her to wash, she could be a model in New York Fashion Week.

She begins to try and push off of the recliner, but lets out a cry and falls back into it. I rush in to help her, wrapping an arm around her. Goosebumps raise across my skin as my arms come into contact with her spine. She's so thin, it's like I'm touching the bones themselves.

Her legs have completely wasted away from three years of disuse.

Even though it makes my head pound in agony, I manage to hold her upright. She weighs practically nothing, which makes my job a little easier.

She's taller than me by a couple of inches, but with the hunch of her back we are about the same height.

I half-drag her toward my apartment—I simply can't let

her stay in this room anymore. Just looking around at this torture chamber makes me feel sick.

Coming up with a plan for next steps will take place in my apartment. It's no room at the Ritz, but at least it isn't *this*.

The journey through the walls takes a few minutes, as my return trip has to take Anya into consideration. She's essentially dead weight in my arms, supported only by my own shaky strength.

Her knobby knees tremble with effort as she tries to step with me. Eventually she gives up in favor of being dragged. Somehow, I manage to get her through the wall without either of us winding up on the floor.

Standing in my living room, I pant as I try to decide what to do next.

I don't have any running water to help Anya clean herself, but I do have some wipes in the bathroom.

We stumble toward the bathroom and push inside. Anya's eyes go wide again as she gets a look at the blood and handcuffs beside the toilet as I lower her down onto it.

"You... escaped?" Anya breathes.

I nod. Then I reach under the sink and pull out the wipes before holding them up so she can see. Anya bows her head in thanks.

It takes a few minutes, but we get her cleaned up before stripping off the dirty rags she's worn for the past three years. I toss them to the floor of the shower and then head for the door to grab some spare clothes for her.

"Please don't... leave me," Anya says, her voice trembling.

I turn around, finding she's stretched out a bony arm as far as she can toward me. There is true desperation in her eyes—she doesn't want to be left behind, left to Claire's devices once again.

BE RIGHT BACK I PROMISE, I scribble onto a sheet of toilet paper that I hold up for her.

I don't have many clothes, but I don't hesitate to share them with Anya. I scoop up a sweatshirt and pair of sweatpants before returning to the bathroom.

Anya has her skeletal arms wrapped around her frame in a pitiful attempt to hold in her body heat. Together we get her clothed, while silent tears drip down her cheeks. I'm crying, too. How could I not?

Once that's done, I help her out of the bathroom and lower her onto my bed. The two of us sit together and catch our breath.

"Thank you," she says.

Her voice is a little stronger than before. I say nothing, only pull her into a hug as I bite my lip to keep from outright weeping. This is no time to fall apart. What this girl has been through is truly awful, but it isn't over.

We hold each other for almost a minute before separating.

Anya lets out another sob and then lowers herself to my sheets, pulling her legs up to her chest until she's in the fetal position.

In another few minutes, she's out cold. I can't imagine how desperate she must be for a decent night of sleep. The wind buffets the windows, drawing my attention away from the girl and back to them.

I think back to my wooden bed fram leg. If I use it to break the glass, I might be able to scream for help. I'm deep in the alley, but there's a small chance someone could hear me.

Anya breathes deeply as she drifts off beside me, her body curled inward like she's still bound. I retrieve the wood leg and grip it tightly between my fingers.

Since Anya is deaf, she won't hear a thing. Squaring up against the first pane of glass, I ready myself. Do I have enough strength left?

All the demolition I did to the drywall, alongside carrying Anya in here, has left me drained. I'm suffering the effects of no food and water, too.

My throat is cracked and dry, feeling like a desert as I swallow painfully. Realizing I have to take care of that first, I slip back through the wall and pick up a few more of Anya's shakes. They go down in seconds, making me feel a little better, but not entirely satiated.

Nothing can replace real food. I imagine that's something Anya understands very well.

Somehow I manage to lift the bed leg with my trembling arm and hurl it into the glass.

The wood slams against it–only to bounce back like it's hit a trampoline. I'm thrown to the floor where I land hard on my elbow, letting out a yelp as spots dance across my vision.

The thing ricocheted and hit me in the head.

I raise my eyes to the windowpane, which rattles ever-so-slightly from the impact. There isn't so much as a scratch.

Of course. Claire had the windows replaced with bullet-proof glass. I should've known she'd think of that.

With a wince, I push myself upright and a glance over at Anya to see if I've disturbed her. She hasn't moved in the slightest.

The windows are out, then. The only one that does open is in Victor's apartment, but the moment I leave my room, Claire will know.

Something tells me I won't be able to get help before she could make it back here. Clamoring to my feet, I force my concussed brain to think. It's soupy now from the lack of food, sleep, and from my injuries.

My gaze returns to Anya laid out atop my covers. Tears prick at the corners of my eyes as I watch her tiny chest rise and fall. How much Claire has taken from her. Her freedom, her body, her hearing.

Then an idea hits me.

An impossibly dangerous idea, but one that just might work.

CHAPTER 38

I t takes me the rest of the night to hammer out the details.
I don't know if I'm hallucinating or just delirious, but
it's the only plan I've got. I can't see another way.

As much as I hate it, the plan requires a couple journeys
back into Anya's torture chamber. By the time I finish prepa-
rations and take a look around, light is filtering in through the
windows. I've gone another night without sleeping.

My stomach is absolutely begging me for food now. Its
persistent cries ring through my head as I sit on the edge of
my bed, hands wrapped absentmindedly around my tummy.

With Anya still asleep, I head back through the wall and
fill up my arms with the meal replacement shakes, bringing
as many as I can carry back to my studio.

I suck down two of them immediately, relishing the taste
as it floods down my throat. The rest of them I put in the
fridge. It's some cheap, no-name store brand, but it's the best
thing I've ever tasted. They help to quench my thirst a
little too.

The only thing to do now is wait for Anya to wake. For
my plan to work, I'll need her. I can only hope she'll have
enough strength to play her part.

My plan is a risky one, but I can't see any alternative. If I sit and wait for Claire to come back like she said she would, she'll discover I've freed Anya and punish us both.

A shiver runs through my body at that thought.

No, we can't afford to wait. The time to act is now.

I have no doubt that when I cross the hall to free Victor, Claire will know. She'll head toward the apartment, and that's when the clock starts ticking.

A pulse of adrenaline kicks through me at the thought of all the things that have to go right. Dark thoughts tear through my brain, their jeering smiles telling me how I'll fail.

Balling my fists, I fight back against the fear. I'm done being taken advantage of. Done.

After another hour, Anya wakes up. She slowly pushes herself upright, shaking like a leaf from the strain of even that much effort. I rush over with a couple more meal replacement shakes in hand.

This time she's able to hold the bottle, though her grip looks weak. I'm ready on standby in case her arm gives out.

As she gulps down the shake, I pull the roll of toilet paper over to me and begin to write.

I HAVE A PLAN TO ESCAPE, I write.

Anya's brown eyes flick over my words. She nods.

It takes me almost five minutes of writing to explain what I need her to do, but once it's finished, I glance up at Anya's face to gauge her thoughts.

Her pale jaw is set in determination. That spark I saw in them yesterday is a fire now, ablaze within the pools of her irises.

"I can do it," she says.

I can tell by her tone of voice she means it. She may be weakened, but she's not out of this fight.

With a nod and another hug, I stand. Now that she knows the plan, it's time for me to get it started.

I finger the paperclip in my pocket. Surprisingly, my hand no longer trembles.

I'm still terrified, yes, but there's something else simmering just behind that feeling. Something deeper and stronger.

Determination.

I can't let Anya and Victor—and the rest of the people trapped in this building—down.

Making my way to the apartment's front door, I pause a moment in the entry hall and settle my breathing. My fingers wrap around the doorknob. Unsurprisingly, it's locked from the outside.

Once I pick this lock and cross the hall, Claire will know something is up. The clock will start. Everything *has* to go perfectly from there on out.

One final breath, and then I drop down to a knee to pick the lock. It doesn't take long to hear the tell-tale click.

Before I can overthink anything, I pull open the door and move across the hallway. As I fall to a knee again and get to work on the lock to Victor's room, my skin feels like it's on fire.

It's like I can *feel* Claire's gaze beating down on my back from the camera in the corner. Who knows how far away she might be? I need to do this as quickly as possible.

My fingers are damp with sweat, and it takes me a little longer than it should to finally get the door unlocked. I swipe a hand across my forehead and open the door inward.

Besides my footsteps on the wooden floorboards, it's absolutely silent. The total lack of noise from the otherwise normal apartment sends a chill down my spine as I race for the couch.

The living area looks completely untouched, almost like no one has ever lived here. I shove the couch to the side to expose the secret door in the wall and press my fingertips against it. In seconds, it's open.

"Victor?" I ask, my voice breathless.

My heart is pounding hard, making my voice quiver a little as I speak. Claire is on her way here.

From my position outside the secret room, I can't get a good look at Victor. He hasn't responded, which makes my heart pound even harder.

Finally there's a rustling of fabric from inside. He's still alive.

"I'm coming in," I say.

Then I'm crawling through the opening, my knees and palms scrambling across the rough flooring before I'm able to stand again.

It's pitch black in here, save for the small slice of light filtering in from the hatch opening.

My eyes need a few moments to adjust, but I can just make out the outline of Victor's sagging figure, his arms suspended overhead in the handcuffs.

"Salem," he says, my name emerging from his dehydrated lips in a broken whisper.

It sounds like he thinks I might be a hallucination. Hurriedly I get to work on the first cuff.

Once it's unlocked, the top part of the cuff drops open and Victor's arm flops out like a ragdoll. He lets out a groan as the entirety of his body weight is being held up by his left shoulder now.

It's tight, but I manage to inch around the front of him to get access to the second cuff. Victor raises his head to look up at me, his dark eyes widening as he realizes this is actually happening.

"How did–"

I shake my head—no time to explain right now. I make quick work of the second handcuff, and finally Victor is free. Slowly, he manages to get to his feet.

For a moment I think he's going to topple forward and

crush me against the wall, but he finds the strength to stand, bracing the wall.

"Can you walk?" I ask.

He swallows and nods. His lips are so dry they're bleeding.

I'm out first, and then Victor ambles through after me. Each of his movements seems to take a tremendous amount of effort, but he manages to crawl out before collapsing on the floor.

"Victor," I say.

"Water," he whispers.

I nod and head for the kitchen. There are a few glasses in the cabinets. I grab one and move to the sink. Mercifully, the water hasn't been cut off to this apartment.

Watching the clear water flow from the tap fills me with a shot of strength. Claire hadn't prepared for this. Didn't expect me to get in here or for Victor to get out. I fill up his glass, my own throat screaming for water as I walk it over to him.

He's propped himself up against the seat of the couch, looking haggard. Victor accepts the glass from me, his large hand shaking a little and spilling a few drops before he tilts it back and gulps down the entire thing.

I'm already back at the sink filling up a glass of my own and thirstily sucking it down. It's just tap water, but I couldn't care less. I've never tasted water so heavenly.

Every sip soothes my parched throat, loosening the baked earth tightness that had stiffened my entire body. The refreshment allows my thoughts to flow freely, like water springing from rock as my thirst is quenched.

Victor staggers back to his feet and joins me at the sink. We alternate filling our glasses and chugging their contents.

Finally we're both satiated, and I set my glass on the counter.

"Claire has cameras in here, she'll know you've gotten

out," Victor says after wiping a massive hand across his mouth.

I nod. "I know. We don't have long. I rescued Anya, too, and—"

"Anya? Where is she?"

Victor's head whips around the room as he looks for her before his shoulders sag downward a little.

"She's in my room," I reply.

His eyes lock in on mine again. "How is she?"

Tears sting the corners of my eyes as I picture Anya's frail body in my mind. I bite my lip, and Victor curses under his breath.

"Listen, Victor, I'm so sorry about everything. Calling the police, and all that," I say, turning his attention back toward me.

"I just... I thought I saw a lot of red flags. I never suspected Claire of anything," I finish.

Victor chews his lip as he nods. "No one ever does. That's how she's gotten away with this for so long."

He looks around again before stalking over to a dresser against the wall. He rips out a stack of books and throws them to the floor. His massive foot comes down atop the stack, and I hear a mechanical crunch as the camera inside them breaks.

"She'll be here soon, I'm sure. We've got to figure out what to do."

"Does the window still open?" I ask.

He moves behind me in the kitchen to stand in front of the window. My breath catches in my throat as Victor places his fingers on the windowsill.

It opens, and cold air rushes in. The window stops in the same place as before.

"You want to try and escape through here?" Victor asks.

"Did it once before."

His eyebrow hikes up in surprise, but it's quickly replaced

by obvious dismay. He shakes his head. "I don't think I'll make it. Even if I could get through the opening, I weigh too much."

It's definitely true. The rickety fire escape could barely hold me when I was out there.

Not to mention the fact that Anya can barely move across a flat surface on her own. The three of us descending the wobbly ladders as they swing in the breeze? Not going to happen.

That's not my escape plan, though. Victor steps aside as I go to the window and slip my body halfway through it.

I shiver as the blast of crisp fall air hits my face. The fire escape twinges below me, rocking ever-so-slightly.

My gaze falls to the rusted bolts holding the slats of the landing in place. They look like with enough pressure, they'd snap clean in half.

I pull my head back inside. "Do you have anything like a hammer in here?"

Victor looks at me questioningly, but walks over to a drawer and pulls out a small hammer before holding it up.

"Here. How is breaking that going to help us? I thought you wanted to escape, not trap yourself here."

"If my plan works, *we* won't be going out there," I reply.

Again, Victor props up an eyebrow. It's clear he has questions, but he's too exhausted and drained to ask them.

With the hammer in hand, I squeeze myself back through the window and start banging away. What I need to do doesn't take long—clearly Claire has little interest in maintaining fire safety codes for the building. That's working in our favor now.

The work is progressing smoothly when I hear Victor shout my name from inside.

I can't see him from the position I'm in, so I scramble for the opening. His tone isn't the kind you ignore.

The back of my head scrapes the bottom of the window as

I drag myself back inside, and I wince as spots dance across my vision.

The pain is the least of my concerns once I spot Victor standing near the other set of windows that face the street.

His face is deathly pale as he stares back at me.

"She's here. She's coming."

CHAPTER 39

Blood pounds in my ears.

Claire is already here. That was way sooner than I'd anticipated—I need more time.

I practically throw myself back out the kitchen window, nearly dropping the hammer in the process before I resume my task.

I have to finish. If I don't, my plan won't work. None of it will.

Behind me, Victor is busy forcing a chair up against the front door, attempting to barricade it. Naturally, Claire has a key. I can hear him grunting and straining as he shoves the leather seat back into position.

"Salem," Victor says, "she just walked inside the building. You need to get out—now."

"I'm not leaving you and Anya behind," I shout over my shoulder.

"It's too late for us. You can make it. Go, now."

The hammer comes down hard one last time, the impact jarring me as well as making my head pulse in agony. But I'm finished.

I pull myself back inside the apartment, my chest rising and falling as I look up at Victor.

"I'm not leaving you to face Claire alone. She'll kill you."

He shakes his head. "I'm sorry I couldn't warn you about her, Salem. It was not my intention to scare you, but I thought if you feared for your life, maybe you'd leave before it was too late."

Victor looks as if he's on the verge of tears. The remaining seconds of our freedom are ticking down quickly now that Claire is in the building.

He's worried about Anya, about me. I can't imagine what this poor man has been through over the past few years.

Footsteps on the tile outside. Both our heads whip toward the hallway as my heartbeat shifts into overdrive.

Is that Claire?

I don't hear anything else, the hallway having gone completely silent.

Victor holds up a large hand, signaling for me to stay where I am as he creeps across the floorboards.

Then a loud pop shatters the air. My hands fly up to cover my ears as I scream in surprise.

Was that a gunshot?

I blink away the spots on my vision and find Victor on the ground, his hands clutching his side.

My mind can't process what I'm looking at, even as the blood begins to pour out from between his fingers.

His mouth drops open, his breath coming in short gasps, the streams of blood spilling out of him making me feel faint.

"You forgot about the camera in the door, Vicky-bear," Claire says from the hallway.

Her saccharine sweet voice spikes my pulse even more as I stare at Victor's blood staining the floor.

He's got his hands pressed tightly to his side, but there's so much blood.

She's watching us through a second camera.

"Now Salem, come unblock this door before I put him down for good, okay?" Claire says in a patient tone worthy of a preschool teacher.

My eyes flick back over to Victor. He's panting, his shoulders rising and falling rapidly. He's propped himself up against the wall, blood pooling around his feet.

I have no choice. I have to let her in. If I don't, Victor is dead and then she'll come for me anyway.

Every footstep feels like a step toward death as I move toward the door.

"Salem," Victor gasps.

He's pleading with me, but I don't know for what. We don't have a choice. Claire will shoot him again if she doesn't get her way, I have no doubt about that.

"There's a good girl," Claire calls out from behind the barricaded door.

Her voice is slightly muffled by the thick wood. My eyes are riveted to the bullet hole marring the surface of the door.

I swallow hard, wondering if Claire will simply shoot me, too, when I open it. Clean house, start over with new "hires."

My fingers wrap around the sides of the chair, and I begin to drag it backward.

The second it's removed from beneath the doorknob, I hear the lock click. The door swings inward to reveal the nightmare that is Claire.

She's all dressed up in a cute fall outfit–a tan trench coat, jeans, and brown suede boots that would blend in at any brunch place in the city. It's the gun in her hand that mars the pretty picture.

Claire flashes her teeth again, but her smile now resembles a wolf baring its fangs. I'm trembling so hard I nearly trip over my own feet as I stumble away from her.

She shuts the door gently behind her then turns toward me, shaking her head back and forth as she *tsk tsks* me.

"Very, very naughty you are," she says.

I continue walking backward until I feel the wall behind me. My heel catches on Victor's pants as he lies sprawled at my feet.

"Did you think I wouldn't find out?" Claire chides. "That I wouldn't stop you?"

I swallow hard, finding speech impossible as she aims the gun at me.

She purses her pouty, painted lips, sliding her gaze to Victor.

"How are you holding up, Vicky-bear?"

He says nothing. For a long moment, his gasping breaths are the only sound breaking the silence.

When Claire straightens again, there's a sick smile spread across her face. The look of it has me paralyzed with fear. She's actually enjoying this.

"I have a fun idea," she says. "It's clear I can't keep the both of you here—that's a recipe for trouble. So why don't you sort that out amongst yourselves?"

I blink.

What is she saying? She wants me and Victor to… kill each other?

"Go ahead, I'll just watch. Victor knows how much I love to watch," she says with a wink.

"Claire, please," Victor gasps from somewhere behind me.

I stumble away from the wall, shaking my head. I don't want to hurt Victor. I won't.

She nudges the gun at him. Her lips curl back in a snarl.

"You'll hurt Salem, or I hurt Anya. I think that's more than fair."

There's the real Claire. The sadistic psychopath who revels in the pain of others.

Victor lets out a groan of agony as he staggers to his feet. He looks like he's about to pass out at any moment.

Our eyes meet. There's so much pain in his dark brown

eyes. Everything he's been through. This will finally break him.

I don't want to hurt him, and he doesn't want to hurt me. Claire waves her hands eagerly, like an impatient child.

"Come on, already. I want to see blood," she whines.

Suddenly there's the sound of heavy footsteps from the hallway, drawing all three of our heads toward the door.

"Salem?"

My heart pounds. That's *Derek*. What's he doing here?

He's outside my door now, knocking hard.

"Salem are you in there? I just want to know that you're okay," he shouts.

He hasn't heard from me in days. In some strange twist of irony, is Derek going to be the one who saves me?

"I'm in here," I shout before Claire can silence me.

CHAPTER 40

Derek is here.

Tall, bearded, slightly-scary Derek.

Claire wouldn't shoot him too, would she?

I throw a look over at her. She's frozen in place, the gun still in hand. She looks as if she's racking her brain for what to do next.

"Salem?" Derek calls again.

"In here Derek, help me," I shout back. "And be careful. She has a gun."

Claire whirls around, waving the weapon wildly as I throw myself down behind the kitchen island.

I hear the door swing open. Derek calls my name again.

"Salem? Is that you? Whose apartment is this? What's—"

The questions cut off abruptly as Derek spots Victor and the blood on the floor around him.

All of us are staring at Derek, and he at us. His gaze shifts around the room, bouncing from person to person.

"Derek, thank you for coming," I say, my words breathless as I push myself back to my feet.

Claire has lowered the gun. Apparently she's unwilling to

shoot a random person, probably because she doesn't control all the variables.

For all she knows, he told someone he was coming here. Someone could report him missing, and the police could track him here. Or check his cell records and follow the trail to the apartment.

We're her playthings, but not Derek. He's a free man.

He takes another step into the room, his eyes wide.

"What happened?" he asks.

Then his gaze falls to the gun in Claire's hand.

"She's insane, she's trapped me here," I say, the words coming out in a rush. "She handcuffed me to the toilet."

Derek blinks and looks around again.

"Are you okay?"

I take a deep breath and nod, just relieved that this horror show is over now. To my surprise however, I find that Derek is shaking his head.

"I wasn't talking to you," he says.

The words are cold, stunning me.

His eyes shift and meet Claire's.

"I was talking to my girlfriend."

CHAPTER 41

*W*hat?

The world feels like it's collapsing around me as Derek crosses the room to stand at Claire's side.

He pulls her into an embrace before kissing her deeply. I can do nothing but stare in stunned silence at the two of them locked together.

Derek's girlfriend.

All the times he mentioned his stupid girlfriend… honestly, I thought she didn't even exist.

But it's been Claire the whole time. I don't know what to think anymore. My knees buckle, and I have to lean against the counter for support.

Derek pulls away from Claire a moment and looks her over.

"I know you told me to wait in the lobby, but I heard the gunshot and got worried, baby," he says.

"I was just having some fun," she replies.

The sight of two of them standing there together makes me want to vomit. I can hardly even think straight. None of this makes sense.

Derek seems to sense my confusion and smiles at me.

"We met on my route. When she told me about the idea of moving the drugs through the trash, I thought it was genius. No one thinks twice about the garbageman," he says.

While she's the brains of this whole scheme, *he's* the arm, enabling the pills produced in the basement to be moved around the city. Derek comes and picks up the trashbags full of pills, and no one is the wiser.

Another realization rocks my body.

"Then that means…" I start, my voice barely above a whisper as it dawns on me.

"It was no accident I found the open room, yeah. Claire mentioned she needed some new blood working in the basement, and I figured you'd be perfect."

I blink hard as the tears begin to pulse at the corners of my eyes. Derek knew *exactly* what went on here when he told me about the apartment. He didn't just happen to come across this place on a garbage route. All of this had been on purpose.

He knew what he was sending me into. My only friend in the city.

The fight drains out of me like water from a broken vase, and I sag more heavily against the counter.

"Kind of makes you wish you'd treated me with a little more respect now, huh?" Derek says with a sneer.

I don't have the strength to reply. Victor has sunk to the floor again, his hands pressed ineffectually against his side. He's growing paler by the second, bleeding out.

"Maybe if you weren't such a tease, we could've worked something out," Derek says. "You could've been a part of the operation, the bigger picture."

My stomach churns as he and Claire both stand there with those putrid smiles plastered across their faces. A matched pair, both of them utterly insane.

"I love you baby," Derek says as he pulls Claire close again.

"Not as much as I love you," she whispers back.

Their noses nuzzle together.

I have no words for what I'm seeing. I don't have any faith left in my plan now either—I didn't for one second factor Derek into any of it.

"I appreciate you checking up on me, sweetums," Claire says as they separate again. "Now that you're here, any input on what we should do with them?"

Derek smiles down at her. "I'm game for whatever you decide, babe. You always have the best ideas."

She beams at him. I grip tight to the countertop so I don't keel over.

Victor looks barely conscious against the wall, his chin sinking lower and lower into his chest.

He's running out of time. So am I.

I don't even want to imagine what sick things Claire will come up with to punish me for breaking free.

Where are you, Anya?

It's all up to her now. My life rests in her fragile hands.

My chest tightens as I picture her passed out again, too weak to enact my plan. If that's the case, I'm as good as dead already.

Claire and Derek both turn toward me. Their predatory gazes make my legs tremble.

"I think I want to put that paperclip she used in her eyeballs," Claire says.

Derek nods. "Great idea, honey. Poetic, even."

They both step toward me in unison, as Claire flashes another vicious smile. My hands come up in front of me. I've got nothing else to defend myself with.

A loud pounding at the door freezes all of us. Claire's head whips over in sync with Derek's. Even Victor stirs and lifts his head.

"This is the police, open up!"

CHAPTER 42

The world bursts into chaos as shouting fills the hallway, more voices demanding for the door to open.

Claire and Derek scramble back farther from the door, clearly in shock.

"How did she call the cops? I thought you took all the phones," Derek hisses at her.

"I *did*," she snaps back.

Her head pivots wildly as she white-knuckles the gun in her hand. Judging from the pounding at the door, the police will be inside at any second. It sounds like there's a whole troop of them out there.

Anya was able to complete her part of the plan.

A gust of wind blows through the open window in the kitchen, the cool air lifting the blonde hair off Claire's face.

I can practically see the gears turning in her mind as she comes to a conclusion.

The fire escape.

Derek sees where she's looking and nods rapidly as the banging starts again.

"Open up, right now," the officer's voice calls.

"That's how Salem got out last time, right? Let's go— hurry," Derek says, pushing Claire toward the open window.

I scramble out of the way as the two of them rush for the window.

More pounding at the door, followed by more shouting.

"Break it down," one of the cops hollers.

Claire is the first to approach the window and stands there a moment as the wind blows in again and rustles her hair.

"What are you doing? They're gonna be in here any second," Derek urges through gritted teeth.

She turns back around.

"You're right. They are. And they need a culprit," she says.

Derek doesn't have time to respond before the bullet buries itself in his chest. He staggers backward, blood pouring from the wound, while Claire slides neatly through the open window.

Derek bounces off the kitchen island and then topples over, his motor function rapidly failing as the blood gushes out.

I leap back to avoid his falling body, and he lands hard on the tile, his head smacking down with a sickening thud.

Looking up at the window, my eyes meet Claire's for a brief second.

She flashes me a smirk before stepping all the way out and disappearing, home free.

Or so she thinks.

A moment later her scream rips the air as the fire escape landing gives way beneath her. I rush to the window and stick my head out, my heart pounding.

Claire is sprawled on the pavement far below, her arms and legs bent at odd angles. The wind blows her brilliantly blonde hair across her face, which is frozen in a wide-eyed death mask.

My eyes drift to the black trash bags sitting in the

alleyway beside her. I watch the breeze ripple across the plastic another moment before pulling my head inside, relief washing over me in powerful waves.

I feel like crying. It's all too much.

I'm filled with an out-of-body sense of unreality as I step back away from the window.

Victor has managed to get himself back to his feet, one hand clutching his side while the other is pressed against the wall. The paint is smeared with his blood, but he's alive.

At my feet, Derek lies motionless, his head facing away from me. I step over him, taking care to avoid the dark blood seeping into the cracks in the tile around him.

"How did you manage to call the cops?" Victor asks.

I shake my head. "I didn't."

Victor's brow furrows in confusion. "Who did then?"

"No one."

I walk down the narrow hallway to the front door, where the sounds of the police pounding on the door continue. It becomes so deafening as I draw near to the door that I wince before pulling it open to reveal the truth.

Anya stands there, her TV remote in hand. Blocking the doorway are two of the floor-standing speakers that sat in her room torturing her for years.

Victor staggers forward.

"I recorded the opening of the cop show Claire forced Anya to listen to every night," I explain, but I'm not sure he hears me.

As if in a daze, he makes his way to the girlfriend he hasn't seen in years—the woman he willingly endured years of torture and abuse to protect.

Victor stares in amazement for a second before Anya's eyes come up to meet his. He freezes. In shock?

In horror at the evidence of the torture she's suffered?

For a moment they only gaze at each other. Then he's

rushing forward, emitting sounds I've never heard from a human as he and Anya finally embrace.

I take a step back, tears filling my eyes as I watch the two of them hug. Victor has his massive arm wrapped around her, sobbing. Anya wails as she grips tight to his blood-soaked shirt.

It's just the two of them.

I did it. It's finally over.

I slide slowly down the wall, drawing in a deep breath as Victor draws Anya inside his apartment where they kiss each other again and again.

"I've missed you so much," he says between wracking sobs, "I didn't know—I didn't—"

Anya nods, tears streaming down her cheeks as she buries her head in his chest.

"My love, my love, my love," she says over and over.

My head pounds. There's blood splattered all over me— Derek's blood. It's seeped into the fabric of my clothes.

My vision swims at the thought. Everything that happened rushes back to me and starts to loop in my mind, until I can't focus on anything but Claire's scream as she fell.

CHAPTER 43

The pounding at the door starts up again.

It's the police, wanting to get in. I can hear their voices as they call out to me through the thick wood of the old door.

Another fist thuds down, but my brain tunes it out until it's little more than background noise. My eyes drift to the wall across from me.

Blood is everywhere. It stains the framed pictures of painted forests, the splattered red running down like tiny river streams before it pools between the old floor tiles.

The cops shout again, their calls frantic as they knock hard.

Even though I know I should open the door, I'm frozen to the spot. My feet won't move. Can't move.

When they come inside, everything will change.

The small window to my left lets in a cool winter breeze, the cold air wafting over my sweat-soaked face and rustling my hair.

My eyes follow the trails of blood down the wall, tracing every inch of the red stains before finally my gaze settles on the body itself.

Here, there's even more blood. Pools of it, the dark liquid sinking deep into every crevice.

I hear the policemen's insistent commands to open the door, but only distantly. I can't pull my eyes away from the body.

So still.

The doorframe shakes as another thunderous boom echoes out in the dingy apartment. Soon, they'll be inside.

Another breeze touches my skin, drawing my gaze toward the open window.

Almost in a trance, I stand slowly and begin taking careful steps toward the window as the cops break through the door behind me.

The wood begins to splinter under the constant assault. I hear them shout my name, but my head doesn't turn.

I reach the window and lower my forehead to it, taking a deep, shaking breath as I peer down to the alleyway below. The glass is cool against my skin.

No doubt there will be alarm when they see the body on the floor.

I just wonder what they'll say when they find out there's another one outside the window, too.

Finally they burst inside, a stream of men brandishing pistols that they sweep over the room.

Victor and Anya look up from their position huddled together on the couch.

"There," Victor croaks, pointing to Derek's body on the floor.

The men continue to sweep inward.

"Salem Ripley?" a man asks as he spots me, his gun lowering.

I nod, unable to speak. It's truly finished. The nightmare is over.

"We got your call," the officer says.

My fingers finally unfurl from Derek's phone. I've had it

clutched in my palm since we called the real police. My hand aches from squeezing it so hard for so long, not wanting to let go of it for fear of never being able to reach the outside world again.

Distantly I hear the officer's gentle voice as he guides me to the couch beside Anya and Victor, both of them under the inspection of paramedics now.

They're checking me out too, pulling open my eyelid as I sit dazedly.

I don't mind—the image of Claire's shattered body outside on the pavement is stuck in my mind, and it's all I can see when my eyes are shut.

Her perfect skin, perfect hair, perfect life. All of it a mask for the darkness that lay beneath.

It's finally over.

Anya is moved onto a stretcher to be transported to the nearest hospital where she'll be treated for severe malnutrition. Victor remains holding her hand the entire time, his eyes never leaving hers.

They're never going to let each other out of their sights again.

The officer is still talking to me, but I can't hear him. There's a distant ringing in my brain as a paramedic bandages my head and guides me up off the couch.

Out of the corner of my eye, I notice they've put Derek on a stretcher too. As they lift him, his arm flops to the side, but I see his chest rise and fall.

He's still alive, somehow.

I'm being helped onto a stretcher of my own. Staring up at the ceiling, all I can think about is how hungry and tired I am. I feel like I've been hit by a truck.

The entire building is swarming with police. Lifting my head as we pass the laundry room, I see an officer step out of the doorway holding a bag packed with white pills.

Everything after that is a blur.

CHAPTER 44

ne month later

O A scream rips through the air, making me jump. Even though I've seen this movie a dozen times, the jump-scares never fail to get me.

Chuckling to myself, I get up off my couch and pad over in my Crocs to the kitchen with a glance at my phone.

Victor and Anya should be here any minute now, and I want to check on the food.

I've started cooking for myself, and I'm finding myself really enjoying it. There's a comforting sense of control that comes from creating a dish from nothing, deciding what does or doesn't go in it.

Cooking has helped me to work through things over the past month. Not completely—still working on it, and it will probably take some time.

When Derek woke up in the hospital, he told the police everything. The drug ring, the slave-labor, the garbage routes. All of it came out, and it was the talk of the city for a couple weeks.

People were amazed something like this could've been happening right under everyone's noses.

I wasn't. It's easy to overlook things when life moves at such a fast pace, as it does in New York City.

Once the media had their fill, they were on to the next story. Of course it's a little harder to move past when you're *part* of the story. I'm trying though.

It took some concentrated effort, but I've been putting myself out there more. Leaving the apartment, seeing the city, meeting people.

That's been good for me—even helped me land my current place, a tiny studio in Hell's Kitchen. Who knew having human connections could be so beneficial?

Dr. DeLuca would be proud of me.

There's a knock at the door. I step away from the stove, where I've got some pasta sauce simmering.

I can hear their voices through the door as I step up to it. Opening it, I greet Victor and Anya with a smile.

They're bundled up against the cold weather, pale faces peeking from between scarves and wool hats.

Both of them are looking much better, Anya especially.

It was a tough period of recovery for her, but she's been able to put on a few pounds. She has to walk with a cane for now while she rebuilds her leg muscles, but knowing her spirit, she'll be free of it soon.

Unfortunately her hearing has been permanently damaged, leaving her mostly deaf—one final parting gift from Claire.

"We brought this," Victor says as he offers a brown bag with a wine bottle inside.

"I hope you like flavor," Anya says in her slightly clipped English.

"I'm sure it's fantastic," I say with a smile as I accept the gift and usher them inside.

The two of them begin stripping off their scarves, hats, and gloves in the warmth in my apartment.

I shut the door and follow them inside.

"Looks good," Victor says with an approving nod as he appraises my place.

I have to admit, I'm proud of it. There isn't a whole lot of stuff in here, but it's filled with things I love. My blanket, my bed, a little desk for me to work at.

There are plenty of plants, too, which fill up the corners of the room and add much needed bursts of color and life to the space.

I'm done with dreary apartments and putting up with *whatever*. It's my space, and I want to be happy in it.

Anya takes a look at the stove.

"What are we having?" she asks.

"Pasta and meatballs," I reply.

Anya looks at me a moment before glancing over at Victor. He uses sign language to sign pasta and meatballs to her, and she gives a satisfied nod.

"I like that," she says with a rub of her belly.

She's still frail, but there's so much life in her. In both of them. As we sit down for dinner, I realize that's not all.

There's still so much life in me, too.

I've got friends now, and I've changed. I'm no longer the girl who gets pushed around.

We all carry scars from our pasts. But as Dr. DeLuca says, sometimes the best thing to do is let go.

———

Thank you so much for reading *The Apartment Across The Hall.* Nothing makes me happier than crafting stories full of twists and turns, and I appreciate you giving my book a chance. I really hope you enjoyed the read.

If you're interested in more psychological thriller good-ness from me, you're invited download a FREE copy of my novella *The Weekend Trip* by heading to jackdanebooks.com and joining my mailing list. That way we can stay in touch, and you'll never miss the news when a new release is happening. I've got some good ones on the way for you!

If you had a great reading experience with this novel, would you take a minute to post a review on Amazon? A few words is all it takes, and it will really make a difference in my career as an author. Reviews are so important in helping other readers find great books that are worth their valuable time and attention.

Reviews are always welcome on Goodreads as well—no pressure of course, only if you have the time.

Thank you again for reading. :)

Jack

ABOUT THE AUTHOR

Jack Dane write thrillers and psychological fiction that largely takes place in New York City, where he lives.

When not writing, Jack enjoys going to jazz clubs, taking people-watching walks in the Park, and exploring the city by night, where he picks up ideas for his next book.

Get a FREE copy of his thriller novella *The Weekend Trip* by heading to jackdanebooks.com

You can connect with Jack on Facebook as well!

Printed in Dunstable, United Kingdom